AN IRREVERSIBLE FATE...

One of the greatest of all the Greek tragedies,
OEDIPUS THE KING *reveals the awesome
impact on the ruler of Thebes of the discovery
that he has been the victim of a terrible
prophecy. Translated into an acting version by
Professor Bernard M. W. Knox, this classic
play by Sophocles is given added dimension
through the clarity of its modernized dramatic
prose.*

The Reader's Supplement to this ENRICHED
CLASSICS edition appears in the center insert.
It has been prepared under the supervision of
an editorial committee directed by Harry
Shefter, Professor of English, New York University, and author of many books used exten-
sively for the improvement of skills in the
language arts. The contributing editor for this
edition was Professor Walter James Miller,
New York University. Grateful acknowledgment
is made to the Picture Collection Division of
the New York Public Library, which provided
much of the illustrative material.

Sophocles
Oedipus the King

Translated by
BERNARD M. W. KNOX

WASHINGTON SQUARE PRESS
PUBLISHED BY POCKET BOOKS NEW YORK

ACKNOWLEDGMENTS

"A venerable Greek philosopher and seer," "Grecian female of the noble class," "Clasps (golden pins) on Greek woman's garment." From *Costumes of the Greeks and Romans* by Thomas Hope, published in 1962, by Dover Publications, Inc.

Caution: Professionals and amateurs are hereby warned that Bernard M. W. Knox's translation of *Oedipus the King*, being fully protected under the copyright laws of the United States of America, the British Empire including the Dominion of Canada, and all other countries of the Copyright Union is subject to a royalty. All rights, including professional, amateur, motion pictures, recitation, public reading, radio and television broadcasting and the rights of translation into foreign languages are strictly reserved. Amateurs may give stage production of this play upon payment of a royalty of twenty dollars for each performance, one week before the play is to be given, to POCKET BOOKS, 1230 Avenue of the Americas, New York, N.Y. 10020.

A Washington Square Press Publication of
POCKET BOOKS, a division of Simon & Schuster, Inc.
1230 Avenue of the Americas, New York, N.Y. 10020

ISBN: 0-671-49946-7

First Pocket Books printing June, 1972

15   14   13   12

FOR BIANCA VANORDEN

ANCIENT GREECE

TRANSLATOR'S PREFACE

This translation is an "acting version." It was made for actors, for a performance; in fact, for the Stratford Shakespearean Festival Company of Canada which filmed a series of lessons on *Oedipus* in color. These films were made by the Council for a Television Course in the Humanities for Secondary Schools, and this translation is intended primarily for those students who will study the play with the aid of the films.

There are so many translations of the *Oedipus* readily available that the reader may wonder why the job had to be done all over again. The reason is that none of the existing translations met the demands of the situation. The films, which are aimed at students in their junior year of high school, required a version which would be immediately intelligible, in performance, to an audience which had

had no previous acquaintance with Greek tragedy and little acquaintance with the theater in any form. The translation had to be clear, simple, direct—its only aim the creation and maintenance of dramatic excitement. To put it another way, it had to be a version which would place no obstacles between the modern audience and the dramatic power of the play.

The translations already available are in verse, with one well-known exception. But most of the verse translations are written by scholars who are not poets, and verse can be a treacherous instrument in the hands of an amateur. It tempts him to indulge in archaic language, in high-sounding obscurities, in cuts and additions dictated by his verse form. On the other hand, the translator who really is a poet tends, for that very reason, to make a poem of his own out of the Greek text and to substitute for the poetic vision of Sophocles his own poetic vision, as Yeats does in his translation of the choral odes of the play. (What would Sophocles have made, for example, of "the Delphic Sybil's trance" or "for Death is all the fashion now, till even Death be dead"?) There is one modern translator, Richmond Lattimore, who is both scholar and poet, and who has given us an *Oresteia* which is both English poetry and an accurate reflection of the original. Unfortunately, he has not translated the *Oedipus*.

There is, of course, the prose translation of Yeats, which has been used in most of the recent performances of the play. But this version has grave disadvantages which do not seem to be generally recognized. Yeats, for reasons he did not see fit to explain, cut the play in the same high-handed way he edited Wilde's *Ballad of Reading Gaol* ("My work gave me that privilege"); what the result is in the case of Wilde I leave to others to judge, but in the case of Sophocles it is close to disastrous. In the last scene of the play, for example, he has omitted ninety of the 226 lines Sophocles wrote, and he has moved parts of speeches as much as a hundred lines away from their true position, not to mention the fact that at one point he has taken two lines from Oedipus, given them to the chorus, and slapped them into the middle of one of Oedipus's long speeches at a point where an interruption destroys the power of the speech. As if this were not enough, he has, in an earlier scene, omitted Jocasta's famous lines on chance, without which the play loses a great deal of its meaning.

So the play had to be translated again. I have used prose (though in some of the choral odes, where the words seem to fall naturally into short lines, I have printed them in that form to suggest the liturgical style of the choral performance. I do not claim that they are verse). The criteria for the prose were clarity and vigor, and in the hope of attaining these two objectives, I have sacrificed everything else. The result is not Sophocles, but I hope that it will give some impression of one dimension of the Sophoclean masterpiece—its dramatic power.

The text of the play is complete; the few minor

omissions of words or phrases are all dictated by the canons of speed and simplicity. In the first scene, for example, Oedipus addresses Creon as "son of Menoeceus." Few people in college, let alone high school, know who Menoeceus was, and the momentary check the strange name gives the audience cuts them off for a moment from the forward movement of the play in which they should be relentlessly involved. So I have dropped Menoeceus and translated simply "Creon." I have heard it argued that even though classical names may be unfamiliar to the modern audience they have a certain dignity and traditional familiarity which creates "atmosphere," but ten years of teaching Greek tragedy in translation have convinced me that to the ordinary American student the name Menoeceus contains no more dignity than the name Lobengula, and is no more familiar; Lobengula in fact has the advantage in that he can pronounce it.

So in many other details. Apollo is sometimes called Loxias in Greek tragedy, and for the Greek poet and audience the use of one name rather than the other sometimes had a point, but actors cannot explain what the point is. In this translation Apollo is always Apollo. And the Delphic oracle is always the Delphic oracle, even if in the Greek it happens to be Pytho. Where the chorus speculates about "enmity between the Labdacids and the son of Polybus," I have translated "Laius and Oedipus." The translation aims to involve in the dramatic impetus of the play an audience which will find it hard enough to acquire even the necessary minimum of basic information. If we have to choose, and I think we do, between making students feel the excitement of the play and making sure they know who Labdacus was, I have no doubt which to choose.

The stage directions all envisage a modern production, not a reconstruction of the original performance. I have taken the liberty of adding a few remarks of a directorial nature where I thought them necessary to bring out the meaning of the passage. I have indicated my belief that the closing lines of the chorus are not part of the Sophoclean original, and at vv. 376-7 I have translated the manuscript reading, not the lines as emended by Brunck. My reasons for all this, and for many other things in the translation, will be found in my *Oedipus at Thebes* (Yale University Press, 1957).

I wish to thank Mr. Douglas Campbell, of the Stratford company, who gave me his expert (and overwhelming) advice on those parts of the translation which are used in the films, and an actress friend (who does not wish to be named) who went over every line of my text to test it for stage delivery. It is because of their patience and generosity that I have the confidence to call this translation an "acting version."

BERNARD M. W. KNOX

OEDIPUS
THE KING

THE CHARACTERS

in the order of their appearance

◇◇◇◇◇◇◇◇◇◇◇◇◇◇◇◇◇◇◇◇◇◇◇◇

OEDIPUS, King of Thebes
A PRIEST of Zeus
CREON, brother of Jocasta
A CHORUS of Theban citizens
TIRESIAS, a blind prophet
JOCASTA, the queen, wife of Oedipus
A MESSENGER from Corinth
A SHEPHERD
A MESSENGER from inside the palace
ANTIGONE
ISMENE } daughters of Oedipus and Jocasta

OEDIPUS THE KING

❖❖❖❖❖❖❖

The background is the front wall of a building,
with a double door in the center. Steps lead
down from the door to stage level. In front
of the steps, in the center, a square stone altar.

❖❖❖❖❖❖❖

[Enter, from the side, a procession of priests and
citizens. They carry olive branches which have tufts
of wool tied on them. They lay these branches on
the altar, then sit on the ground in front of it. The
door opens. Enter Oedipus.]

OEDIPUS

My sons! Newest generation of this ancient city
of Thebes! Why are you here? Why are you seated
there at the altar, with these branches of supplication?

I

The city is filled with the smoke of burning incense, with hymns to the healing god, with laments for the dead. I did not think it right, my children, to hear reports of this from others. Here I am, myself, world-famous Oedipus.

You, old man, speak up—you are the man to speak for the others. In what mood are you sitting there—in fear or resignation? You may count on me; I am ready to do anything to help. I would be insensitive to pain, if I felt no pity for my people seated here.

PRIEST

Oedipus, ruler of Thebes, you see us here at your altar, men of all ages—some not yet strong enough to fly far from the nest, others heavy with age, priests, of Zeus in my case, and these are picked men from the city's youth. The rest of the Thebans, carrying boughs like us, are sitting in the market place, at the two temples of Athena, and at the prophetic fire of Apollo near the river Ismenus.

You can see for yourself—the city is like a ship rolling dangerously; it has lost the power to right itself and raise its head up out of the waves of death. Thebes is dying. There is a blight on the crops of the land, on the ranging herds of cattle, on the still-born labor of our women. The fever-god swoops down on us, hateful plague, he hounds the city and empties the houses of Thebes. The black god of death is made rich with wailing and funeral laments.

It is not because we regard you as equal to the gods that we sit here in supplication, these children and I; in our judgment you are first of men, both in the normal crises of human life and in relations with the gods.

You came to us once and liberated our city, you freed us from the tribute which we paid that cruel singer, the Sphinx. You did this with no extra knowledge you got from us, you had no training for the task, but, so it is said and we believe, it was with divine support that you restored our city to life. And now, Oedipus, power to whom all men turn, we beg you, all of us here, in supplication—find some relief for us! Perhaps you have heard some divine voice, or have knowledge from some human source. You are a man of experience, the kind whose plans result in effective action. Noblest of men, we beg you, save this city. You must take thought for your reputation. Thebes now calls you its savior because of the energy you displayed once before. Let us not remember your reign as a time when we

3

stood upright only to fall again. Set us firmly on our feet. You brought us good fortune then, with favorable signs from heaven—be now the equal of the man you were. You are king; if you are to rule Thebes, you must have an inhabited city, not a desert waste. A walled city or a ship abandoned, without men living together inside it, is nothing at all.

OEDIPUS

My children, I am filled with pity. I knew what you were longing for when you came here. I know only too well that you are all sick—but sick though you may be, there is not one of you as sick as I. *Your* pain torments each one of you, alone, by himself—by my spirit within me mourns for the city, and myself, and all of you. You see then, I was no dreamer you awoke from sleep. I have wept many tears, as you must know, and in my ceaseless reflection I have followed many paths of thought. My search has found one way to treat our disease—and I have acted already. I have sent Creon, my brother-in-law, to the prophetic oracle of Apollo, to find out by what action or speech, if any, I may rescue Thebes. I am anxious now when I count the days since he left; I wonder what he is doing. He has been away longer than one would expect,

4

longer than he should be. But when he comes, at that moment I would be a vile object if I did not do whatever the god prescribes.

PRIEST

Just as you say these words, these men have signaled to me to announce Creon's arrival.

[*Enter Creon, from side.*]

OEDIPUS

[*Turns to the altar*] O King Apollo! May Creon bring us good fortune and rescue, bright as the expression I see on his face.

PRIEST

I guess that his news is joyful. For on his head is a crown of laurel in bloom.

OEDIPUS

No more guessing—soon we shall know. For he is near enough to hear us now.

[*Raising his voice*] Lord Creon, what statement do you bring us from the god Apollo?

5

CREON

Good news. For, as I see it, even things hard to bear, if they should turn out right in the end, would be good fortune.

OEDIPUS

What exactly did the god say? *Your* words inspire neither confidence nor fear.

CREON

If you wish to hear my report in the presence of these people [*Points to priests*] I am ready. Or shall we go inside?

OEDIPUS

Speak out, before all of us. The sorrows of my people here mean more to me than any fear I may have for my own life.

CREON

Very well. Here is what I was told by the god Apollo. He ordered us, in clear terms, to drive out the thing that defiles this land, which we, he says, have fed and cherished. We must not let it grow so far that it is beyond cure.

6

OEDIPUS

What is the nature of our misfortune? How are we to rid ourselves of it—by what rites?

CREON

Banishment—or repaying blood with blood. We must atone for a murder which brings this plague-storm on the city.

OEDIPUS

Whose murder? Who is the man whose death Apollo lays to our charge?

CREON

The ruler of this land, my lord, was called Laius. That was before *you* took the helm of state.

OEDIPUS

I know—at least I have heard so. I never saw the man.

CREON

It is to *his* death that Apollo's command clearly refers. We must punish those who killed him—whoever they may be.

7

OEDIPUS

But where on earth are they? The track of this ancient guilt is hard to detect; how shall we find it now?

CREON

Here in Thebes, Apollo said. What is searched for can be caught. What is neglected escapes.

OEDIPUS

Where did Laius meet his death? In his palace, in the countryside, or on some foreign soil?

CREON

He left Thebes to consult the oracle, so he announced. But he never returned to his home.

OEDIPUS

And no messenger came back? No fellow traveler who saw what happened?

CREON

No, they were all killed—except for one, who ran away in terror. But he could give no clear account of what he saw—except one thing.

8

OEDIPUS

And what was that? One thing might be the clue to knowledge of many more—if we could get even a slight basis for hope.

CREON

Laius was killed, he said, not by one man, but by a strong and numerous band of robbers.

OEDIPUS

But how could a *robber* reach such a pitch of daring—to kill a king? Unless there had been words —and money—passed between him and someone here in Thebes.

CREON

We thought of that, too. But the death of Laius left us helpless and leaderless in our trouble—

OEDIPUS

Trouble? What kind of trouble could be big enough to prevent a full investigation? Your *king* had been killed.

9

CREON

The Sphinx with her riddling songs forced us to give up the mystery and think about more urgent matters.

OEDIPUS

But I will begin afresh. I will bring it all to light. You have done well, Creon, and Apollo has, too, to show this solicitude for the murdered man. Now you will have *me* on your side, as is only right. I shall be the defender of Thebes, and Apollo's champion, too. I shall rid us of this pollution, not for the sake of a distant relative, but for my own sake. For whoever killed Laius might decide to raise his hand against me. So, acting on behalf of Laius, I benefit myself, too.

[*To priests*] Quickly, my children, as fast as you can, stand up from the steps and take these branches of supplication off the altar.

[*To guards*] One of you summon the people of Thebes here.

I shall leave nothing undone. With God's help we shall prove fortunate—or fall.

10

PRIEST

My sons, stand up. [*The priests rise.*] King Oedipus has volunteered to do what we came to ask. May Apollo, who sent the message from his oracle, come as our savior, and put an end to the plague.

[*The priests take the olive branches off the altar and exeunt to side. Oedipus goes back through the palace doors. Enter, from side, the chorus. They are fifteen dancers, representing old men. They stand for the people of Thebes, whom Oedipus has just summoned. They chant in unison the following lines, which, in the original Greek, make great use of solemn, traditional formulas of prayer to the gods.*]

CHORUS

Sweet message of Zeus! You have come from Apollo's golden temple to splendid Thebes, bringing us news. My fearful heart is stretched on the rack and shudders in terror.

Hail Apollo, Lord of Delos, healer! I worship and revere you. What new form of atonement will you demand? Or will it be some ancient ceremony, repeated often as the seasons come round? Tell me, daughter of golden Hope, immortal Voice of Apollo.

First I call upon you, immortal Athena, daughter of Zeus. And on your sister Artemis, the protector of this land, who sits in glory on her throne in the market place. And I call on far-shooting Apollo, the archer. Trinity of Defenders against Death, appear to me! If ever in time past, when destruction threatened our city, you kept the flame of pain out of our borders, come now also.

There is no way to count the pains we suffer. All our people are sick. There is no sword of thought which will protect us. The fruits of our famous land do not ripen. Our women cannot ease their labor pains by giving birth. One after another you can see our people speed like winged birds, faster than irresistible fire, to the shore of evening, to death. The city is dying, the deaths cannot be counted. The children lie unburied, unmourned, spreading death. Wives and gray-haired mothers come from all over the city, wailing they come to the altar steps to pray for release from pain and sorrow. The hymn to the Healer flashes out, and with it, accompanied by flutes, the mourning for the dead. Golden daughter of Zeus, Athena, send help and bring us joy.

I pray that the raging War-god, who now without shield and armor hems me in with shouting and burns me, I pray that he may turn back and leave the borders of this land. Let him go to the great sea gulf of the Western ocean or north to the Thracian coasts which give no shelter from the sea. For now, what the night spares, he comes for by day.

Father Zeus, you that in majesty govern the blazing lightning, destroy him beneath your thunderbolt!

Apollo, king and protector! I pray for the arrows from your golden bow—let them be ranged on my side to help me. And with them the flaming torches of Artemis, with which she speeds along the Eastern mountains. And I invoke the god with the golden headdress, who gave this land his name, wine-faced Dionysus, who runs with the maddened girls—let him come to my side, shining with his blazing pine-torch, to fight the god who is without honor among all other gods.

[*The chorus stays on stage. Enter Oedipus, from the palace doors. He addresses the chorus—the people of Thebes.*]

13

OEDIPUS

You are praying. As for your prayers, if you are willing to hear and accept what I say now and so treat the disease, you will find rescue and relief from distress. I shall make a proclamation, speaking as one who has no connection with this affair, nor with the murder. Even if I had been here at the time, I could not have followed the track very far without some clue. As it is, I became a Theban citizen with you after it happened. So I now proclaim to all of you, citizens of Thebes: whoever among you knows by whose hand Laius son of Labdacus was killed, I order him to reveal the whole truth to me.

If he is afraid to speak up, I order him to speak even against himself, and so escape the indictment, for he will suffer no unpleasant consequence except exile; he can leave Thebes unharmed.

[*Silence while Oedipus waits for a reply.*]

Secondly, if anyone knows the identity of the murderer, and that he is a foreigner, from another land, let him speak up. I shall make it profitable for him, and he will have my gratitude, too.

[*Pause.*]

14

But if you keep silent—if someone among you refuses my offer, shielding some relative or friend, or himself—now, listen to what I intend to do in that case. That man, whoever he may be, I banish from this land where I sit on the throne and hold the power; no one shall take him in or speak to him. He is forbidden communion in prayers or offerings to the gods, or in holy water. Everyone is to expel him from their homes as if he were himself the source of infection which Apollo's oracle has just made known to me. That is how I fulfill my obligations as an ally to the god and to the murdered man. As for the murderer himself, I call down a curse on him, whether that unknown figure be one man or one among many. May he drag out an evil death-in-life in misery. And further, I pronounce a curse on myself if the murderer should, with my knowledge, share my house; in that case may I be subject to all the curses I have just called down on these people here. I order you all to obey these commands in full for my sake, for Apollo's sake, and for the sake of this land, withering away in famine, abandoned by heaven.

Even if this action had not been urged by the god, it was not proper for you to have left the matter unsolved—the death of a good man and a

15

king. You should have investigated it. But now I am in command. I hold the office he once held, the wife who once was his is now mine, the mother of my children. Laius and I would be closely connected by children from the same wife, if his line had not met with disaster. But chance swooped down on his life. So I shall fight for him, as if he were my own father. I shall shrink from nothing in my search to find the murderer of Laius, of the royal line of Thebes, stretching back through Labdacus, Polydorus and Cadmus, to ancient Agenor. On those who do not co-operate with these measures I call down this curse in the gods' name: let no crop grow out of the earth for them, their wives bear no children. Rather let them be destroyed by the present plague, or something even worse. But to you people of Thebes who approve of my action I say this: May justice be our ally and all the gods be with us forever!

CHORUS

[*One member of the chorus speaks for them all.*]

You have put me under a curse, King, and under the threat of that curse I shall make my statement. I did not kill Laius and I am not in a position to say who did. This search to find the murderer should have been undertaken by Apollo who sent the message which began it.

OEDIPUS

What you say is just. But to compel the gods to act against their will—no man could do that.

CHORUS LEADER

Then let me make a second suggestion.

OEDIPUS

And a third, if you like—speak up.

CHORUS LEADER

The man who sees most eye to eye with Lord Apollo is Tiresias and from him you might learn most clearly the truth for which you are searching.

OEDIPUS

I did not leave *that* undone either. I have already sent for him, at Creon's suggestion. I have sent for him twice, in fact, and have been wondering for some time why he is not yet here.

17

CHORUS LEADER

Apart from what he will say, there is nothing but old, faint rumors.

OEDIPUS

What were they? I want to examine every single word.

CHORUS LEADER

Laius was killed, so they say, by some travelers.

OEDIPUS

I heard that, too. Where is the man who saw it?

CHORUS LEADER

If he has any trace of fear in him, he won't stand firm when he hears the curses you have called down on him.

OEDIPUS

If he didn't shrink from the action he won't be frightened by a word.

18

CHORUS LEADER

But here comes the one who will convict him.
These men are bringing the holy prophet of the
gods, the only man in whom truth is inborn.

[*Enter Tiresias, from the side. He has a boy to
lead him, and is accompanied by guards.*]

OEDIPUS

Tiresias, you who understand all things—those
which can be taught and those which may not be
mentioned, things in the heavens and things which
walk the earth! You cannot see, but you understand the city's distress, the disease from which it
is suffering. You, my lord, are our shield against
it, our savior, the only one we have. You may not
have heard the news from the messengers. We sent
to Apollo and he sent us back this answer: relief
from this disease would come to us only if we dis-
covered the identity of the murderers of Laius and
then either killed them or banished them from
Thebes. Do not begrudge us your knowledge—any
voice from the birds or any other way of prophecy
you have. Save yourself and this city, save me,
from all the infection caused by the dead man. We
are in your hands. And the noblest of labors is for

a man to help his fellow men with all he has and can do.

TIRESIAS

Wisdom is a dreadful thing when it brings no profit to its possessor. I knew all this well, but forgot. Otherwise I would never have come here.

OEDIPUS

What is the matter? Why this despairing mood?

TIRESIAS

Dismiss me, send me home. That will be the easiest way for both of us to bear our burden.

OEDIPUS

What you propose is unlawful—and unfriendly to this city which raised you. You are withholding information.

TIRESIAS

I do not see that your talking is to the point. And I don't want the same thing to happen to me.

20

OEDIPUS

If you know something, in God's name, do not turn your back on us. Look. All of us here, on our knees, beseech you.

TIRESIAS

You are all ignorant. I will never reveal my dreadful secrets, or rather, yours.

OEDIPUS

What do you say? You know something? And will not speak? You intend to betray us, do you, and wreck the state?

TIRESIAS

I will not cause pain to myself or to you. Why do you question me? It is useless. You will get nothing from me.

OEDIPUS

You scoundrel! You would enrage a lifeless stone. Will nothing move you? Speak out and make an end of it.

TIRESIAS

You blame my temper, but you are not aware of one *you* live with.

OEDIPUS

[*To chorus*]

Who could control his anger listening to talk like this—these insults to Thebes?

TIRESIAS

What is to come will come, even if I shroud it in silence.

OEDIPUS

What is to come, *that* is what you are bound to tell *me*.

TIRESIAS

I will say no more. Do what you like—rage at me in the wildest anger you can muster.

OEDIPUS

I will. I am angry enough to speak out. I understand it all. Listen to me. I think that *you* helped to plan the murder of Laius—yes, and short of actually raising your hand against him you did it. If you weren't blind, I'd say that you alone struck him down.

TIRESIAS

Is that what you say? I charge you now to carry out the articles of the proclamation you made. From now on do not presume to speak to me or to any of these people. *You* are the murderer, *you* are the unholy defilement of this land.

OEDIPUS

Have you no shame? To start up such a story! Do you think you will get away with this?

TIRESIAS

Yes. The truth with all its strength is in me.

OEDIPUS

Who taught you this lesson? You didn't learn it from your prophet's trade.

TIRESIAS

You did. I was unwilling to speak but you drove me to it.

23

OEDIPUS

What was it you said? I want to understand it clearly.

TIRESIAS

Didn't you understand it the first time? Aren't you just trying to trip me up?

OEDIPUS

No, I did not grasp it fully. Repeat your statement.

TIRESIAS

I say that you are the murderer you are searching for.

OEDIPUS

Do you think you can say that twice and not pay for it?

TIRESIAS

Shall I say something more, to make you angrier still?

OEDIPUS

Say what you like. It will all be meaningless.

TIRESIAS

I say that without knowing it you are living in shameful intimacy with your nearest and dearest. You do not see the evil in which you live.

OEDIPUS

Do you think you can go on like this with impunity forever?

TIRESIAS

Yes, if the truth has power.

OEDIPUS

It has, except for you. You have no power or truth. You are blind, your ears and mind as well as eyes.

TIRESIAS

You are a pitiful figure. These reproaches you fling at me, all these people here will fling them at you—and before very long.

25

OEDIPUS

[*Contemptuously*]

You live your life in one continuous night of darkness. Neither I nor any other man that can see would do you any harm.

TIRESIAS

It is not destiny that I should fall through you. Apollo is enough for that. It is *his* concern.

OEDIPUS

Was it Creon, or you, that invented this story?

TIRESIAS

It is not Creon who harms you—you harm yourself.

OEDIPUS

Wealth, absolute power, skill surpassing skill in the competition of life—what envy is your reward! For the sake of this power which Thebes entrusted to me—I did not ask for it—to win this power faithful Creon, my friend from the beginning, sneaks up on me treacherously, longing to drive me out. He sets this intriguing magician on me, a lying quack, keen sighted for what he can make, but blind in prophecy.

[*To Tiresias*] Tell me, when were you a true prophet? When the Sphinx chanted her riddle here, did *you* come forward to speak the word that would liberate the people of this town? That riddle was not for anyone who came along to answer—it called for prophetic insight. But you didn't come forward, you offered no answer told you by the birds or the gods. No. *I* came, know-nothing Oedipus, *I* stopped the Sphinx. I answered the riddle with my own intelligence—the birds had nothing to teach me. And now you try to drive me out, you think you will stand beside Creon's throne. I tell you, you will pay in tears for this witch-hunting— you and Creon, the man that organized this con- spiracy. If you weren't an old man, you would al- ready have realized, in suffering, what your schemes lead to.

CHORUS LEADER

If we may make a suggestion—both his words and yours, Oedipus, seem to have been spoken in anger. This sort of talk is not what we need—what we must think of is how to solve the problem set by the god's oracle.

27

TIRESIAS

King though you are, you must treat me as your equal in one respect—the right to reply. That is a power which belongs to me, too. I am not your servant, but Apollo's. I am not inscribed on the records as a dependent of Creon, with no right to speak in person. I can speak, and here is what I have to say. You have mocked at my blindness, but you, who have eyes, cannot see the evil in which you stand; you cannot see where you are living, nor with whom you share your house. Do you even know who your parents are? Without knowing it, you are the enemy of your own flesh and blood, the dead below and the living here above. The double-edged curse of your mother and father, moving on dread feet, shall one day drive you from this land. You see straight now but then you will see darkness. You will scream aloud on that day; there is no place which shall not hear you, no part of Mount Cithaeron here which will not ring in echo, on that day when you know the truth about your wedding, that evil harbor into which you sailed before a fair wind.

There is a multitude of other horrors which you do not even suspect, and they will equate you to yourself and to your own children. There! Now smear me and Creon with your accusations. There is no man alive whose ruin will be more pitiful than yours.

OEDIPUS

Enough! I won't listen to this sort of talk from you. Damn you! My curse on you! Get out of here, quickly. Away from this house, back to where you came from!

TIRESIAS

I would never have come here if you had not summoned me.

OEDIPUS

I didn't know that you were going to speak like a fool—or it would have been a long time before I summoned you to my palace.

TIRESIAS

I am what I am—a fool to you, so it seems, but the parents who brought you into the world thought me sensible enough. [*Tiresias turns to go.*]

OEDIPUS

Whom do you mean? Wait! Who is my father?

TIRESIAS

This present day will give you birth and death.

29

OEDIPUS

Everything you say is the same—riddles, obscurities.

TIRESIAS

Aren't you the best man alive at guessing riddles?

OEDIPUS

Insult me, go on—but that, you will find, is what makes me great.

TIRESIAS

Yet that good fortune was your destruction.

OEDIPUS

What does that matter, if I saved Thebes?

TIRESIAS

I will go, then. Boy, lead me away.

OEDIPUS

Yes, take him away. While you're here you are a hindrance, a nuisance; once out of the way you won't annoy me any more.

30

TIRESIAS

I am going. But first I will say what I came here to say. I have no fear of you. You cannot destroy me. Listen to me now. The man you are trying to find, with your threatening proclamations, the murderer of Laius, that man is here in Thebes. He is apparently an immigrant of foreign birth, but he will be revealed as a native-born Theban. He will take no pleasure in that revelation. Blind instead of seeing, beggar instead of rich, he will make his way to foreign soil, feeling his way with a stick. He will be revealed as brother and father of the children with whom he now lives, the son and husband of the woman who gave him birth, the murderer and marriage-partner of his father. Go think this out. And if you find that I am wrong, then say I have no skill in prophecy.

[*Exit Tiresias led by boy to side. Oedipus goes back into the palace.*]

CHORUS

Who is the man denounced by the prophetic voice from Delphi's cliffs—the man whose blood-stained hands committed a nameless crime? Now is the time for him to run, faster than storm-swift horses. In full armor Apollo son of Zeus leaps upon him, with the fire of the lightning. And in the murderer's track follow dreadful unfailing spirits of vengeance.

The word of Apollo has blazed out from snowy Parnassus for all to see. Track down the unknown murderer by every means. He roams under cover of the wild forest, among caves and rocks, like a wild bull, wretched, cut off from mankind, his feet in pain. He turns his back on the prophecies delivered at the world's center, but they, alive forever, hover round him.

The wise prophet's words have brought me terror and confusion. I cannot agree with him, nor speak against him. I do not know what to say. I waver in hope and fear; I cannot see forward or back. What cause for quarrel was there between Oedipus and Laius? I never heard of one in time past; I know of none now.

I see no reason to attack the great fame of Oedipus in order to avenge the mysterious murder of Laius.

Zeus and Apollo, it is true, understand and know in full the events of man's life. But whether a mere man knows the truth—whether a human prophet knows more than I do—who is to be a fair judge of that? It is true that one man may be wiser than another. But I, for my part, will never join those who blame Oedipus, until I see these charges proved. We all saw how the Sphinx came against him—there his wisdom was proved. In that hour of danger he was the joy of Thebes. Remembering that day, my heart will never judge him guilty of evil action.

[*Enter Creon, from side.*]

CREON

Fellow citizens of Thebes, I am here in an angry mood. I hear that King Oedipus brings terrible charges against me. If, in the present dangerous situation, he thinks that I have injured him in any way, by word or deed, let me not live out the rest of my days with such a reputation. The damage done to me by such a report is no simple thing—it is the worst there is—to be called a traitor in the city, by all of you, by my friends.

CHORUS LEADER

This attack on you must have been forced out of him by anger; he lost control of himself.

CREON

Who told him that *I* advised Tiresias to make these false statements?

CHORUS LEADER

That's what was said—but I don't know what the intention was.

CREON

Were his eyes and mind unclouded when he made this charge against me?

CHORUS LEADER

I don't know. It is no use asking *me* about the actions of those who rule Thebes. Here is Oedipus. Look, he is coming out of the palace.

[*Enter Oedipus, from door.*]

OEDIPUS

[*To Creon*]

You! What are you doing here? Do you have the face to come to my palace—you who are convicted as my murderer, exposed as a robber attempting to steal my throne? In God's name, tell me, what did you take me for when you made this plot—a coward? Or a fool? Did you think I wouldn't notice this conspiracy of yours creeping up on me in the dark? That once I saw it, I wouldn't defend myself? Don't you see that your plan is foolish—to hunt for a crown without numbers or friends behind you? A crown is won by numbers and money.

CREON

I have a suggestion. You in your turn listen to a reply as long as your speech, and, after you have heard me, *then* judge me.

OEDIPUS

You are a clever speaker, but I am a slow learner—from *you*. I have found you an enemy and a burden to me.

CREON

Just one thing, just listen to what I say.

OEDIPUS

Just one thing, don't try to tell me you are not a traitor.

35

CREON

Listen, if you think stubbornness deprived of intelligence is a worth-while possession, you are out of your mind.

OEDIPUS

Listen, if you think you can injure a close relative and then not pay for it, you are out of your mind.

CREON

All right, that's fair. But at least explain to me what I am supposed to have done.

OEDIPUS

Did you or did you not persuade me that I ought to send for that "holy" prophet?

CREON

Yes, I did, and I am still of the same mind.

OEDIPUS

Well then, how long is it since Laius ... [*Pause.*]

CREON

Did what? I don't follow your drift.

OEDIPUS

Disappeared, vanished, violently murdered?

CREON

Many years ago; it is a long count back in time.

OEDIPUS

And at that time, was this prophet at his trade?

CREON

Yes, wise as he is now, and honored then as now.

OEDIPUS

Did he mention my name at that time?

CREON

No, at least not in my presence.

OEDIPUS

You investigated the murder of Laius, didn't you?

37

CREON

We did what we could, of course. But we learned nothing.

OEDIPUS

How was it that this wise prophet did not say all this *then?*

CREON

I don't know. And when I don't understand, *I* keep silent.

OEDIPUS

Here's something you *do* know, and could say, too, if you were a loyal man.

CREON

What do you mean? If I know, I will not refuse to answer.

OEDIPUS

Just this. If he had not come to an agreement with you, Tiresias would never have called the murder of Laius *my* work.

CREON

If that's what he says—you are the one to know.
Now I claim my rights from you—answer my questions as I did yours just now.

OEDIPUS

Ask your questions. I shall not be proved a murderer.

CREON

You are married to my sister, are you not?

OEDIPUS

The answer to that question is yes.

CREON

And you rule Thebes jointly and equally with her?

OEDIPUS

She gets from me whatever she wants.

CREON

And I am on an equal basis with the two of you, isn't that right?

39

OEDIPUS

Yes, it is, and that fact shows what a disloyal friend you are.

CREON

No, not if you look at it rationally, as I am explaining it to you. Consider this point first—do you think anyone would prefer to be supreme ruler and live in fear rather than to sleep soundly at night and still have the same power as the king? I am not the man to long for royalty rather than royal power, and anyone who has any sense agrees with me. As it is now, I have everything I want from you, and nothing to fear; but if I were king, I would have to do many things I have no mind to. How could the throne seem more desirable to me than power and authority which bring me no trouble? I can see clearly—all I want is what is pleasant and profitable at the same time. As it is now, I am greeted by all, everyone salutes me, all those who want something from you play up to me —that's the key to success for them. What makes you think I would give up all this and accept what you have? No, a mind which sees things clearly, as I do, would never turn traitor. I have never been tempted by such an idea, and I would never have put up with anyone who took such action.

You can test the truth of what I say. Go to Delphi and ask for the text of the oracle, to see if I gave you an accurate report. One thing more. If you find that I conspired with the prophet Tiresias, then condemn me to death, not by a single vote, but by a double, yours and mine both. But do not accuse me in isolation, on private, baseless fancy. It is not justice to make the mistake of taking bad men for good, or good for bad. To reject a good friend is the equivalent of throwing away one's own dear life—that's my opinion. Given time you will realize all this without fail: time alone reveals the just man —the unjust you can recognize in one short day.

CHORUS LEADER

That is good advice, my lord, for anyone who wants to avoid mistakes. Quick decisions are not the safest.

OEDIPUS

When a plotter moves against me in speed and secrecy, then I too must be quick to counterplot. If I take my time and wait, then his cause is won, and mine lost.

CREON

What do you want then? Surely you don't mean to banish me from Thebes?

OEDIPUS

Not at all. Death is what I want for you, not exile.

CREON

You give a clear example of what it is to feel hate and envy.

OEDIPUS

You don't believe me, eh? You won't give way?

CREON

No, for I can see you don't know what you are doing.

OEDIPUS

Looking after my own interests.

CREON

And what about mine?

42

OEDIPUS

You are a born traitor.

CREON

And you don't understand anything.

OEDIPUS

Whether I do or not—I am in power here.

CREON

Not if you rule badly.

OEDIPUS

[*To Chorus*]

Listen to him, Thebes, my city.

CREON

My city, too, not yours alone.

CHORUS LEADER

Stop, my lords. Here comes Jocasta from the house, in the nick of time. With her help, you must compose this quarrel between you.

43

[*Enter Jocasta, from door.*]

JOCASTA

Have you no sense, God help you, raising your voices in strife like this? Have you no sense of shame? The land is plague-stricken and you pursue private quarrels. [*To Oedipus*] You go into the house, and you, too, Creon, inside. Don't make so much trouble over some small annoyance.

CREON

Sister, your husband, Oedipus, claims the right to inflict dreadful punishments on me. He will choose between banishing me from my fatherland and killing me.

OEDIPUS

Exactly. Jocasta, I caught him in a treacherous plot against my life.

CREON

May I never enjoy life, but perish under a curse, if I have done to you any of the things you charge me with.

44

JOCASTA

In God's name, Oedipus, believe what he says.
Show respect for the oath he swore by the gods—
do it for my sake and the sake of these people here.

CHORUS

Listen to her, King Oedipus. Think over your
decision, take her advice, I beg you.

OEDIPUS

What concession do you want me to make?

CHORUS

Creon was no fool before, and now his oath in-
creases his stature. Respect him.

OEDIPUS

Do you know what you are asking?

CHORUS

Yes, I know.

OEDIPUS

Tell me what it means, then.

CHORUS

This man is your friend—he has sworn an oath—
don't throw him out dishonored on the strength of
hearsay alone.

OEDIPUS

Understand this. If that is what you are after,
you want me to be killed or banished from this land.

CHORUS

No. By the sun, foremost of all the gods! May I
perish miserably abandoned by man and God, if
any such thought is in my mind. My heart is racked
with pain for the dying land of Thebes—must you
add new sorrows of your own making to those we
already have?

OEDIPUS

Well then, let him go—even if it *does* lead to my
death or inglorious banishment. It is *your* piteous
speech that rouses my compassion—not what *he*
says. As for him, I shall hate him, wherever he goes.

CREON

You show your sulky temper in giving way,
just as you did in your ferocious anger. Natures like

OEDIPUS THE KING

SOPHOCLES (496–406 B.C.)

BIOGRAPHICAL BACKGROUND

Sophocles, son of Sophillus, was born at Colonus, just outside Athens, around 496 B.C. He came of a well-to-do family and was given the education of a young aristocrat of the period, which included athletics and music. As a boy, he led the chorus that sang a hymn of thanksgiving to the gods at the celebration for the great naval victory of Salamis, in 480 B.C., which saved Greece from the Persian invader and launched the city of Athens on a brilliant career of political and economic expansion. His long life stretched over the entire span of the great age of Athens and ended in 406 B.C., just two years before the city surrendered to the Spartans at the close of the long and disastrous Peloponnesian War.

During his ninety years he played a distinguished part in public affairs, as general on at least one occasion, and as a member of a special commission of ten that was chosen to guide Athens through the desperate years that followed the loss of the fleet in Sicily (413 B.C.). But he was known to his fellow citizens mainly as the most successful dramatist who had ever presented plays in the theater of Dionysus. He won his first victory at the tragic festival in 468 B.C., defeating the older poet Aeschylus. He was then twenty-eight years old. This was the start of a career which was to bring him the first prize in the contest no less than eighteen times; he was sometimes awarded the second prize (as in the year when he produced *Oedipus the King*), but never, we are told, the third.

Sophocles wrote 123 plays. Only seven of them have come down to us complete. These are: *Ajax* (probably the earliest of his plays to have survived), *Antigone* (produced in 442 B.C.), *Oedipus the King* (some time between 430 and 411 B.C.), *Philoctetes* (409 B.C.), *Oedipus at*

Colonus (produced after his death in 406 B.C.), and the *Electra* and *Trachiniae,* whose dates are quite uncertain. Among these seven plays, *Oedipus the King* is generally regarded as the dramatic masterpiece not only of Sophocles but also of the whole magnificent range of ancient tragedy.

—Bernard M. W. Knox

HISTORICAL BACKGROUND

1. *Ancient Athens*

Athens in the fifth century B.C. was by modern standards a small and uncomfortable city. The total population of Athens and its surrounding territory, Attica, was probably not more than three hundred thousand, and the city itself was crowded, dirty, and from a material point of view, primitive—the Athenians had no running water in their houses, no central heating, no adequate artificial light. And yet it was in this city and at this time that the foundations of our modern Western civilization were firmly laid. In fifth-century Athens, European philosophy, history, drama, architecture, and sculpture emerged full-grown in masterpieces which have been dominating examples ever since.

The incredible achievements of the Athenians of the fifth century will probably never be satisfactorily explained, but there are certain historical factors which help us to understand why the human spirit was so enormously energetic and creative in this particular time and place. Early in the century (490–479 B.C.), the Greeks, weak, poor, and divided, had astonished the world (and themselves) by beating off a large-scale attempt at conquest by the forces of the Persian Empire, an Eastern despotism which controlled the resources of a land empire stretching from the borders of Greece to those of India. The Greeks, and particularly the Athenians, who had played a decisive role in the Persian defeat, were inspired by a new heroic vision of their own potentialities; if they had beaten off the Persian army and fleet, there was nothing they could not do. In Athens, especially, the result of the victory was a fantastic burst of energy which showed itself not only in political and naval offensive action against Persia on its home ground, but also in every domain of civic and private endeavor.

It so happened that Athens possessed a form of government particularly adapted to encourage and guide this new-found energy. Athens was a democracy, the first in the history of the world. Its institutions allowed and even demanded a freedom of thought and discussion which was the best possible soil for the growth of new ideas, new forms of action and achievement.

It was a kind of democracy that is possible only in a small community; it worked not through representatives, as ours does, but through an assembly of the whole citizen body—a town meeting, in fact. There was, of course, a council, a committee that prepared the agenda for the town meeting, and there were executive officials who carried on the day-to-day business of government. All of these officials were elected by the assembly every year, and the same man could not be immediately elected for a second term—except to the vital office of general, where, obviously, once a good man was found, the best thing was to keep him in the job. Pericles, the guiding spirit of Athens during its great period, was elected general year after year, and in this office directed the foreign and domestic policies of Athens. Sophocles himself was elected one of the ten generals on at least one occasion and actually commanded naval units in the campaign. According to a humorous anecdote that has come down to us, he was a better strategist at the banquet table than at sea, and this by his own admission.

Athens was a democracy but, as hostile critics have often pointed out, democratic rights were not extended to the slaves. There were slaves, of course, in great numbers—probably eighty thousand in Attica as a whole. They did the heavy work of the society—in the silver mines, on the land, in the houses. They had no share in the rule of the people (which is what is meant by the Greek word *demokratia,* from which "democracy" is derived), no voice in the town meeting.

Yet there is much evidence to show that slaves were treated better at Athens than anywhere else (and it must be remembered that all ancient civilizations were based on slave labor). In fact, an anti-democratic writer complained that at Athens slaves would not make way for you on the street and you were not allowed to strike them. The reason for this, he added maliciously, was that since free men and slaves looked exactly alike, you would often find that the slave you had started to beat was a free Athenian citizen. In any case, it must be remembered that the development of full democracy has been a slow and painful business; it is remarkable enough that Athens invented democracy for its free population so long before this form of government appeared elsewhere. And we Americans should be especially tolerant on this point, for when the great documents of our own democratic faith, the Declaration of Independence and the Constitution, were drafted and signed, many of the colonies were slave states and many of the signers were slave owners, a fact to which the slave quarters at Mount Vernon still bear eloquent testimony.

The small free population and the town-meeting form of government allowed the Athenian to take a much greater part in public affairs than we do today. He acted in person rather than through representatives and senators. And this was true also in the court of law, where he could not hire a lawyer, but had to state his own case himself, before a jury of his fellow citizens. He probably would have been very active in this sphere, for the Athenians were only too ready to sue each other. He also acted for himself in sports, which the Greeks, like us, followed with passionate interest. There were professional athletes, of course, but most of the competitors at the great Greek games—the Olympics, for example—were amateurs, ordinary citizens who had become experts in the athletic exercises which every young Athenian practiced as a matter of course.

The Athenian of Sophocles' time was thus forced, by the circumstances of his life, to act in person in many situations where today the citizen turns to the expert, and this meant that his interest in all the questions of the day was not academic, but practical and passionate. And this interest was not confined to political and economic questions. The writers, artists, and philosophers of Athens, unlike their counterparts today who appeal to a select minority, found a mass audience which was quick to react, to understand, to criticize. This may help to explain the tremendous steps forward which were taken in the arts and many other allied fields in Athens in the fifth century B.C.

2. *The Theater of Dionysus*

In addition to democracy, the Athenians invented the theater. Its origins in Greece are lost in the dark of early history; the fifth-century Athenians themselves probably could not have explained how the theater started. But by the time of Sophocles, it was flourishing in Athens, a regular part of the communal life of the city. We do know that it began as a dance. The oldest element of the Athenian drama was a chorus, and the chorus was a group of dancers—*chorus,* in Greek, means "dance," not "song," a meaning still preserved in the word "choreography." The drama began as a dance connected with the worship of the god Dionysus; it was a ceremony of worship, performed on a circular dancing floor. The original dance was probably a fairly primitive affair, like other dances in other times and places which have been danced in honor of a god—in Africa, in Australia, and also in America among the Indians. Such dancers often wear masks, to make them look like animals, perhaps the animal associated with the god they are worshiping, and in Athens in the fifth century the dancers still wore masks.

Though dances like this are common among primitive peoples all over the world, only in one place—Athens—did they turn into drama. How it happened we shall probably never know, but it is possible to guess. The masked chorus danced and sang, its subject some story about Dionysus. Somebody at some point added to the dance of the chorus another masked performer who did not dance or sing, but spoke, and who gave the chorus some new information or answered its questions. This was the first actor or, as the Greeks called him, *hypokrites,* a term formed from the Greek word that originally meant "to answer" and, in the later sense of "actor," has given us the word "hypocrite." The name of the experimental genius who added the first actor to the dance was, according to the Greeks, Thespis and, if he did nothing else, his name deserves to be remembered. For if one actor, why not two? And with two actors, we have the beginning of drama as we know it; the two actors can actually represent Dionysus and one of his companions, or even two characters not connected with Dionysus at all. If two actors, why not three? The dramatist who added a third actor was Sophocles himself.

In the late fifth century, when *Oedipus the King* was first produced, the theater was still a religious place, and the performance was an act of worship of the god Dionysus, the god of all living, growing things, and especially of the vine. The plays were presented at his annual festival, which took place in the early spring. In Athens you could not go to the theater whenever you wanted to; it was active only during the three-day festival of Dionysus. But when the Athenians did go to the theater, they took it seriously. They went at sunrise and sat through three tragedies, a short farcical play which had a chorus of satyrs (the half-bestial companions of Dionysus), and a comedy. They did this for three days in succession. The three tragedies and the satyr play performed on any one day were all by the same poet, though a different poet wrote the comedy. At the end of the festival, prizes were awarded by a board of judges, who would naturally take their cues from the reactions of the audience; the three tragic and the three comic poets were awarded first, second, and third prizes. The first prize was a crown of ivy. The playwright did not expect to make any money out of the performance of his play, nor did the producer, who was a wealthy man paying the expenses of the performance as a public service. There was a charge for admission, but it was very small, and citizens who could not afford to pay it were given free tickets.

The audience was not a select group; it was the Athenian people as a whole, all of them who could get away from home obligations or military service. The theater had a capacity of fourteen thousand. The audience began making its way to the theater before dawn—the old men leaning on their sticks as they walked, the soldiers from the walls, the young men from wealthy families who could afford horses to serve in the cavalry and ride in the state processions, the working population, potters, masons, farmers from just outside the city, sailors from ships in the harbor, the women who made the clothes and prepared the food for the family, the boys from the wrestling school— all of them came, bringing a cushion to sit on (marble benches seem hard after a few hours) and food to munch during the intervals between the plays, or during the plays if they weren't very exciting. They were a very lively audience, likely to burst into tears if the play was powerful and well acted, or to hiss and whistle if they didn't like it.

What they saw from their seats in the open air was not what we expect to see in the theater. From the marble

benches they could see the circular dancing floor and
behind it the stage building, with doors and perhaps col-
umns, which would represent a palace or a temple and
from which the masked actors would make an "entrance."
There was no curtain, no lighting; the simple scenery con-
sisted mostly of props—a statue or an altar. A trumpet
call gave the signal for silence and attention, and after it,
the play began with the appearance of a masked actor or
with the chorus marching past the stage building to its
position on the dancing floor. The audience had no pro-
gram to tell them the dramatic time and place, no list of
the cast of characters. The opening lines of the play had
to make clear the identity of the characters, the place and
time, and the situation. This was easily and economically
done, since the play was nearly always based on a story
already well known to the audience; a few hints would be
enough to set the stage action in the framework of the
story as the audience already knew it.

The masks worn by the chorus and actors seem to have
been fairly standardized. There were recognizable types—
old man, middle-aged man, youth, old woman, and so on.
For *Oedipus the King,* a special mask probably had to be
made for the entry of Oedipus after he has put out his
eyes. The masks, like all full-face masks, would naturally
exaggerate the size of the face, but they were not the
grotesque exaggerations sometimes pictured in handbooks
and on modern theater curtains. The artificially heightened
hair over the forehead which most modern reproductions
show is now generally agreed to be an innovation of the
Greek theater of a much later day than that of Sophocles,
and the popular idea that the mouth of the mask was a
funnel that acted as a megaphone has no basis in fact.
The masks certainly ruled out the play of facial expression
which we regard today as one of the actor's most important
skills, but in the theater of Dionysus, where even the front
row of spectators was sixty feet away from the stage (the

back rows were three hundred feet away), facial expression could not have been seen anyway. And the masks had a practical value. They made it possible for the same actor to play two or even three or four different parts in different scenes of the play—a useful arrangement in Athens, where trained actors whose voices could reach the rear rows of the immense audience were scarce and expensive. In *Oedipus the King,* all the speaking parts were played by three actors. A probable arrangement was: one actor for Oedipus; another for the priest, Jocasta, the shepherd, and the messenger from inside the house; and the third actor for Creon, Tiresias, and the Corinthian messenger.

The dress of the actors was, according to literary authorities and contemporary vase paintings, ornate and magnificent. But the still widespread idea that the actors wore a sort of elevator shoe that gave them abnormal height and prevented any fast or natural movement is almost certainly not true for the theater of Sophocles, though such boots were used later when the level of the stage was raised.

It is still widely believed that the fifth-century dramatists were bound by the so-called "classical" unities of place and time, and that they tastefully avoided blood and horror on the stage. Such ideas have no basis in fact. First, change of scene, though difficult because of the presence of the chorus, was possible in the Greek theater—the scenes are changed in the *Ajax* of Sophocles and the *Eumenides* of Aeschylus. Second, there are many places in the surviving plays where long intervals of dramatic time separate one scene from another. And last, the spectators in the theater of Dionysus were treated to many a violent and horrific spectacle—Ajax impales himself on his sword; Philoctetes, suffering from an ulcerated foot, screams in agony, falls into delirium and finally into unconsciousness; Evadne throws herself on the burning

funeral pyre of her husband; Prometheus has an iron
wedge driven through his chest; and Oedipus, in our play,
comes out of the palace feeling his blinded way, his face
running with blood. The Athenian audience was a mass
audience, and the Athenian dramatists, like Shakespeare
after them, learned how to combine the subtlest poetic use
of language with the unashamed exploitation of strong
visual effects.

There is one aspect of the performance that remains
strange to us in spite of every effort of the historical imag-
ination; it is always the least successful feature of modern
revivals of the plays. This is the chorus. Early in the play
a group of twelve or fifteen masked dancers came marching out to take up their positions on the circular dancing
floor in front of the stage building. They remained there
until the end of the play. And at intervals during the play,
usually with the stage area cleared of actors, they danced
and at the same time sang, to a flute accompaniment, a
choral ode. These odes were written in complicated meters
and ornate, complex, lyrical language; their content was
liturgical and reflective rather than dramatic. The choral
odes were, like the masks, a legacy from the original form
of worship out of which the drama evolved, and in the
later years of the fifth century, especially in those plays of
Euripides which abandoned tragic themes and concentrated
on the sheer excitement of a melodramatic, romantic plot,
they were treated frankly as musical interludes between
the scenes played by the actors. But Sophocles used
them with the utmost poetic and dramatic skill to illustrate,
discuss, and set in a broader social and religious context
the actions and speeches of the characters in the play.

The choral odes in *Oedipus the King* are a brilliant
example of what a dramatic genius was able to do with an
obstinately undramatic form. The first chorus, a prayer to
the gods, brings home to us, in a way individual actors
could never do, the reality of the plague as seen through

the eyes of a whole people. The second presents us with the agonized reflections of the people of Thebes on the accusations and counteraccusations of Oedipus and Tiresias; a people sits in judgment on its ruler. In the third the chorus points up and explores for us the great issue raised by the action—the truth or falsity of divine prophecy—and in closing lines full of dramatic tension takes its stand for the truth of divine prophecy and, therefore, against Oedipus and Jocasta. The fourth ode shows us the chorus in a moment of feverish excitement and exaltation as it expresses its hopes that the secret of the birth of Oedipus, soon to be revealed, will bring glory to him and to Thebes —a magnificently ironic prelude to the tremendous scene of discovery that follows. And in the last ode, facing the full and dreadful truth, the chorus presents the fate of Oedipus as an image of man's rise and fall in words which for solemn beauty and terrifying grandeur have no equal in European literature.

—Bernard M. W. Knox

LEGEND AND IRONY IN GREEK DRAMA

Sophocles and his fellow dramatists used for their plays stories of a time long past which were the familiar heritage of all Athenians—stories they had learned from their parents and would pass on to their children in turn. To a large extent, then, the element of novelty, which is characteristic of the modern theater, was missing, though the stories were so rich in variants and so flexible in detail that minor surprises were possible and were often provided. But what the dramatist lost in novelty he gained in other ways. The myths he used gave to his plays, without any effort on his part, some of those larger dimensions of authority which the modern dramatist must create out of nothing if his play is to be more than a passing entertainment. The myths had the authority of history, for myth is in one of its aspects the *only* history of an age that kept no records. They had also the authority inherent in moral and religious symbols, for the myths served as typical patterns of the conduct of man and the manifestation of the gods. They were stories in which the historical, moral, and religious experience of the whole race was distilled.

The myths gave the ancient dramatist another advantage One of the most difficult problems facing the modern dramatist—exposition, the indication early in the play of the background of the characters and their situation—was, for the ancient dramatist, no problem at all. He had only to indicate the identity of the characters and the point in the story where his play began, and the job was done. He could limit his exposition to emphasizing those particular details of the background which were important for his own treatment of the story.

The audience, once it recognized the story, knew what had preceded the action of the play. But it knew even more. It knew more or less accurately what was going to happen in the play itself. And this fact enabled the ancient dramatist to work in a vein which is characteristic of Greek tragedy and especially of Sophocles—dramatic irony. Everything said by the characters in the play means more to the audience than it does to the speaker. For the audience knows more than he does, knows the truth about the past (which Oedipus, for example, does not know) and the truth about the future. The audience during the play is in fact in the position of the gods, and is able to see the struggles, hopes, and fears of the characters against a background of the truth—past, present, and future. This situation gives to the dramatic action as a whole an intensity and complication which are the hallmark of Greek tragedy; the audience understands everything on two different levels at once. It is involved emotionally in the blind heroic efforts of Oedipus, a man like each of them; and it is detached from those efforts by its superior knowledge, the knowledge of the gods. Ancient tragedy gives the spectator an image of his own life, not only as he sees it and lives it himself, but as it must look to the all-seeing eye of divine knowledge.

This somber irony shows itself not only in the larger frame of the action but in details, too. One speech after another in the play uses the audience's knowledge to provide a dramatic shock: Jocasta's speech to Oedipus on her first entrance, with its scolding, nagging tone that suggests a mother reproving a wayward son; the answer of the chorus to the Corinthian messenger, "This lady is . . . his wife and mother of his children"; Oedipus's statement that he will fight on behalf of Laius "as if he were my own father"—all these dramatic hammer blows are made possible by the fact that the audience knows the story to begin with.

The story is old, strange, and terrible. Laius and Jocasta, the childless king and queen of Thebes, were told by the god Apollo that their son would kill his father and marry his mother. A son was born to them, and they tried to make sure that the prophecy would not come true. Laius drove a metal pin through the infant's ankles and gave it to a shepherd, with instructions to leave it to die of exposure on the nearby mountain, Cithaeron. The shepherd took the child up to the mountain, but pitied it and gave it to a fellow shepherd he met there, who came from Corinth, on the other side of the mountain range. This shepherd took the child with him and gave it to the childless king and queen of Corinth, Polybus and Merope. They brought the child up as their own son, and named him Oedipus, which in its Greek form *Oidipous* means "swollen foot" (his feet had been injured by the metal pin). So Oedipus grew up in Corinth as the king's son, with no idea of his real parentage. And Laius and Jocasta believed that their child was dead and the prophecy of Apollo false.

After Oedipus became a young man, he was told, by a man who had drunk too much at a banquet, that he was not the real son of Polybus. He was reassured by Polybus and Merope, but a lingering doubt remained and rumors were spreading abroad. He went, on his own initiative, to Delphi, in the north of Greece, to the oracle of Apollo, to ask the god who his parents were. All he was told was that he would kill his father and marry his mother. He resolved never to return to Corinth, to Polybus and Merope, and started out to make a new life for himself elsewhere. He came to a place where three main roads met, and in the narrow place was ordered off the road and then attacked by the driver of a chariot in which an old man was riding. A fight started, and Oedipus, in self-defense, killed the old man and his attendants—all except one, who escaped and took the news to Thebes. The old man in the chariot was Laius, king of Thebes. And so the first half of the prophecy of Apollo was fulfilled. Oedipus, though he did not know it, had killed his father.

Oedipus continued on his way and came to Thebes. He found the city in distress. A monster, the Sphinx—part bird, part lion, part woman—was killing the young men of Thebes and refused to go away until someone answered her riddle. Many had tried, but all failed, and met their death. The Thebans offered a great reward to anyone who could answer the riddle of the Sphinx—the throne of Thebes and the hand of Jocasta, the widowed queen, in marriage. Oedipus volunteered to answer the riddle: "There is a creature two-footed, and also four-footed, and three-footed. It has one voice. When it goes on most feet, then it goes most slowly." Oedipus answered the riddle correctly. The answer is Man, who goes on all fours as a child, on two feet as an adult, and on three as an old man, since he has a stick to help him along.

Oedipus married Jocasta and became king of Thebes. The prophecy was fulfilled, but he did not realize it. For many years he ruled Thebes well, an admired and just king. He had two daughters and two sons. And then a plague broke out in Thebes. The people of the city died, the cattle died, the crops rotted. The Thebans thronged the temples, and a delegation of priests went to the palace to beg Oedipus to save them. These are the priests who come on stage at the beginning of the play, and as they enter, the stage door opens and a masked actor comes out and addresses them. The play has begun.

—Bernard M. W. Knox

Note: The page references on the following pages direct your attention to passages in the text (T for Top of page, M for Middle, and B for Bottom).

PICTORIAL BACKGROUND

OEDIPUS

The city is filled with the smoke of burning incense, with hymns to the healing god, with laments for the dead. I did not think it right, my children, to hear reports of this from others. Here I am, myself, world-famous Oedipus. (p. 2T)

STREET SCENE IN ANCIENT GREECE

PRIEST
I guess that his news is joyful. For on his head is a crown of laurel in bloom. (p. 5M)

A "CROWN" OR WREATH OF LAUREL WORN AS A
SYMBOLIC HEAD DECORATION

CREON

Very well. Here is what I was told by the god Apollo. He ordered us, in clear terms, to drive out the thing that defiles this land, which we, he says, have fed and cherished. We must not let it grow so far that it is beyond cure. (p. 6B)

A VERSION OF THE GOD APOLLO

The priests take the olive branches off the altar and exeunt to side. Oedipus goes back through the palace doors. Enter, from side, the chorus. (p. 11M)

A TYPICAL CHORUS IN A GREEK THEATER

CHORUS

Sweet message of Zeus! You have come from Apollo's golden temple to splendid Thebes, bringing us news. My fearful heart is stretched on the rack and shudders in terror. (p. 11M)

ZEUS (JUPITER) ON HIS THRONE—THE TEMPLE AT OLYMPIA (RECONSTRUCTED)

CHORUS

First I call upon you, immortal Athena, daughter of Zeus.
And on your sister Artemis, the protector of this land, . . .
And I call on far-shooting Apollo, the archer. Trinity of
Defenders against Death, appear to me! (p. 12T)

A BRONZE STATUE OF ATHENA (MINERVA)

CHORUS

Apollo, king and protector! I pray for the arrows from your golden bow—let them be ranged on my side to help me. And with them the flaming torches of Artemis, with which she speeds along the Eastern mountains. (p. 13M)

ARTEMIS (DIANA), APOLLO'S TWIN SISTER

CHORUS

And I invoke the god with the golden headdress, who gave this land his name, wine-faced Dionysus, who runs with the maddened girls—let him come to my side, shining with his blazing pine-torch . . . (p. 13M)

DIONYSUS (BACCHUS), GOD OF WINE AND REVELRY

OEDIPUS

Tiresias, you who understand all things—those which can be taught and those which may not be mentioned, things in the heavens and things which walk the earth! You cannot see, but you understand the city's distress, . . . (p. 19M)

A VENERABLE GREEK PHILOSOPHER AND SEER

OEDIPUS

I came, know-nothing Oedipus, I stopped the Sphinx. I answered the riddle with my own intelligence—the birds had nothing to teach me. And now you try to drive me out, you think you will stand beside Creon's throne. I tell you, you will pay in tears for this witch-hunting—you and Creon, . . . (p. 27M)

A GREEK VERSION OF A SPHINX

CHORUS

Who is the man denounced by the prophetic voice from Delphi's cliffs—the man whose blood-stained hands committed a nameless crime? Now is the time for him to run, faster than storm-swift horses. (p. 31B)

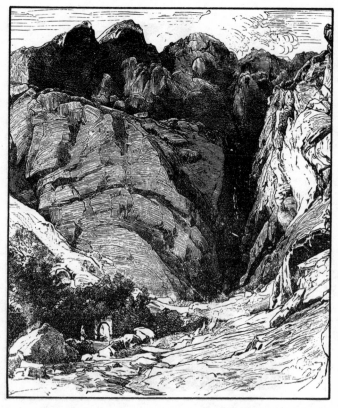

THE DELPHI CLIFFS (SKETCHED FROM NATURE)

JOCASTA

Have you no sense, God help you, raising your voices in strife like this? Have you no sense of shame? The land is plague-stricken and you pursue private quarrels. [To Oedipus] *You go into the house, and you, too, Creon, inside. (p. 44T)*

GRECIAN FEMALE OF THE NOBLE CLASS

OEDIPUS

I will tell you the truth, all of it. As I journeyed on I came near to this triple crossroad and there I was met by a herald and a man riding on a horse-drawn wagon, just as you described it. The driver, and the old man himself, tried to push me off the road. In anger I struck. . . . (p. 56B)

A GREEK CHARIOT (FROM A VASE PAINTING)

CORINTHIAN MESSENGER

The people of Corinth will make Oedipus their king, so I heard there.

JOCASTA

What? Is old Polybus no longer on the throne?

CORINTHIAN MESSENGER

No. He is dead and in his grave. (p. 64T)

CORINTH IN HELLENIC TIMES

CORINTHIAN MESSENGER

No wonder he doesn't remember, master. He forgets, but I'll remind him, and make it clear. I am sure he knows very well how the two of us grazed our flocks on Cithaeron—he had two and I only one—we were together three whole summers, . . . (p. 83M)

GREEK SHEPHERD BEFORE MOUNT OLYMPUS

MESSENGER

*And when the poor woman was lying on the ground—
then we saw the most dreadful sight of all. He ripped out
the golden pins with which her clothes were fastened,
raised them high above his head, and speared the pupils of
his eyes. "You will not see," he said, "the horrors I have
suffered. . . ." (p. 93M)*

CLASPS (GOLDEN PINS) ON GREEK WOMAN'S GARMENT

MESSENGER

He is shouting, "Open the doors, someone: show me to all the people of Thebes, my father's killer, my mother's" —*I cannot repeat his unholy words. He speaks of banishing himself from Thebes, says he will not remain in his house under the curse which he himself pronounced. (p. 94M)*

INTERIOR OF REGAL GRECIAN HOME

OEDIPUS

*Children, where are you? Come here, . . . I weep for you
—see you I cannot—when I think of your future, the
bitter life you will lead, the way men will treat you. What
gatherings will you go to, what festivals, without returning
home in tears, instead of taking part in the ceremonies?
(p. 104B)*

GREEK GIRLS AT PLAY—A PART OF LIFE OEDIPUS
BELIEVES IS NOW DENIED TO HIS DAUGHTERS

CRITICAL EXCERPTS

Selected from the hundreds of articles, biographies, and volumes of criticism written about Sophocles, here are some excerpts that should prove challenging to you. We have included page references to *Oedipus the King* (in parentheses) so that you can review the passages indicated to help you decide whether to accept or reject the quoted comments.

1. *It sometimes happens that a great poet creates a character in whom the essence of an age is distilled, a representative figure who in his action and suffering presents to his own time the image of its victory and defeat. For later centuries this character becomes the central reference point for an understanding of his creator's time; but he is a figure of such symbolic potency that he appears to them not only as a historical but also as a contemporary phenomenon. The poet who created him has penetrated so deeply into the permanent elements of the human situation that his creation transcends time. One such figure is Hamlet, Prince of Denmark, and such another is Oedipus, King of Thebes.*

> *Oedipus at Thebes*, Bernard Knox,
> Yale University Press, 1957.

2. *Aristotle and most subsequent critics regard* Oedipus . . . *as the model Greek tragedy. Each step in the intricate and perfectly dovetailed plot is motivated, and none seems contrived; the inherent improbabilities in the received story are made unobtrusive. The delineation of even the minor characters is perfect; witness the contrast between the voluble Corinthian and the reluctant shepherd. The choral odes are apposite and beautiful. The tragedy is centered in Oedipus and grows out of the interaction of his own impetuous character and destiny. The force of the tragic irony is terrific as Oedipus becomes the last person in the*

whole theater to realize the devastating truth. In a drama so perfectly wrought as to make us oblivious of its author, we cannot say that this or that line expresses the author's own conviction. Yet there may be significance in the choice of a theme which demonstrates the infallibility of Apollo's oracle and in which the tragic flaw is immoderate passion.

> *A History of Greek Literature,* Moses Hadas, Columbia University Press, 1950.

3. *. . . . everyone who reads or sees the play remarks on the excellence of the plot construction. There is indeed an unremitting progress towards the goal, enlivened by moments when the truth seems certain to emerge. So steady is this progress that the play has established a sort of standard for all time. If we think of drama in general, the* Oedipus *is more akin to our ideals than any other tragedy the Greeks produced. . . .*

> *Sophocles the Playwright,* S. M. Adams, University of Toronto Press, 1957.

4. *Sophocles produced in* King Oedipus *the masterpiece of his life's work, so far as we can judge from the seven plays surviving out of the hundred or more ascribed to his pen. This is the judgment also of Aristotle, who has this play constantly at his elbow as the perfect type of tragic composition. In brief, its greatness lies in the combination of a faultlessly articulated plot with the profoundest insight into human motive and circumstance. . . .*

> *Sophocles: The Theban Plays,* E. F. Walting, Penguin Books, 1947.

These comments get us off to a good start by reminding us of the valuable services that critics perform for us. They inform us of the *reputation* of the work of art. Completely aside from our own opinions and reactions, we do want to know—as a *historical fact*—how the work is generally regarded. And here we learn that four critics picked at random speak of *Oedipus* in superlative terms—*great, perfect, beautiful, ideal, faultless*—and they tell us that these opinions are typical of critics both ancient and modern.

5. . . . *the Greek theatre was religious, not commercial . . . What the Greeks wrote were, from our point of view, not much more than long one-act plays: they take little over an hour, at most an hour and a half, to perform . . . a chorus that sings and dances is found in all works written by major playwrights. The reader must keep in mind, must remember that the serious plays were part grand opera and the comedies part musicals.*

> *Classical Age*, Lionel Casson, Editor, Dell Publishing Co., 1965.

6. *Jocasta's . . . treatment of her newborn son would not revolt the audience, for exposure of unwanted children was both frequent and legal in Athens.*

> *The Life and Work of Sophocles*, F. J. H. Letters, Sheed and Ward, 1953.

7. *Oedipus* tyrannos, *then, is more than an individual tragic hero. In his title,* tyrannos, *in the nature and basis of his power, in his character, and in the mode of his dramatic action, he resembles Athens, the city which aimed to become (and was already far along the road to becoming) the* tyrannos *of Greece, the rich and splendid autocrat of the whole Hellenic world. Such a resemblance, whether consciously recognized or not, must have won him the sympathy of the Athenian audience and firmly engaged the emotions of that audience in the hero's action and suffering. But it does something more. It adds an extra dimension of significance not only to his career but also to his fall, which suggests, in symbolic, prophetic, riddling terms, the fall of Athens itself. Like*

Oedipus, Athens justifies unceasing and ever more vigorous action by an appeal to previous success; like Oedipus, Athens refuses to halt, to compromise, to turn back; like Oedipus, Athens follows the dictates of her energy and intelligence with supreme confidence in the future; and like Oedipus, the tragedy seems to suggest, Athens will come to know defeat, learn to say "I must obey" as she now says "I must rule." Athens, in the words of her greatest statesman, claimed that she was an example to others . . . Oedipus is called an example too, but in his fall.

Oedipus at Thebes, Bernard Knox.

Such historical information is valuable indeed. Horrified as we might be today over Jocasta's acknowledgment of infanticide (p. 50M), we are forced to regard the practice in terms of the times (p. 88M). And notice how helpful it is to have this historical context copiously supplied in colorful comparisons . . . Greek tragedy resembles our opera! And Dr. Knox's comments show us a whole dimension of appreciation of the play that is inaccessible to us unless we know ancient history well . . . or read his fascinating book. Here are a few passages from critics who have tried to explain the appeal of tragic drama:

8. *A perfect tragedy should . . . imitate actions which excite pity and fear . . . and through pity and fear, effect the proper purgation of these emotions . . . the change of fortune presented . . . should be that of a man who is not eminently good and just, yet whose misfortune is brought about not by vice or depravity, but by some error or frailty. He must be one who is highly renowned and prosperous—a personage like Oedipus . . . or other illustrious men of such families . . . the plot ought to be so constructed that, even without the aid of the eye, he who hears the tale told will thrill with horror and melt to pity at what takes place. This is the impression we should receive from hearing the story of the Oedipus.*

Poetics, Aristotle, Dover Publications, 1951.

9. *In reading or witnessing the* Oedipus Tyrannus, *we are not possessed with a fear that we may be placed in circumstances similar to those of Oedipus, or be overtaken by the same calamities. Yet a thrill runs through us, a shudder of horror or of vague foreboding. The feeling is immediate and unreflective. The tension of mind, the agonized expectation with which we await the impending catastrophe, springs from our sympathy with the hero in whose existence we have for the time merged our own.*

> *Aristotle's Theory of Poetry and Fine Art,* S. H. Butcher, Editor, Dover Publishing Co., 1951.

10. . . . *have we not overstressed the "fall" as a tragic element even in the older drama? Is not attrition, or the "breaking down" process, actually an element in such plays as* Oedipus the King, King Lear, *and* Macbeth? *I have been more deeply stirred by the manner in which Oedipus is deprived of his certainties and Lear is worn out as a human being than by a precipitate fall from greatness. It is not that they are hurled down like Lucifer from heaven but that they crumble in some fundamental respect, as many men do, that moves me most. And I should have been so moved, I suspect, even if Oedipus had not gouged out his eyes at the end and Lear had not died. To be ground down is the most universal—the only truly universal—destiny. It can also be made just as pitiful and fear-inspiring as physical destruction.*

> "Aristotelian Literary Criticism," John Gassner, in *Aristotle's Theory of Poetry and Fine Art,* S. H. Butcher, Editor.

Explanations of the play's emotional appeal given above are typical of those offered by *literary* critics. Now consider another famous passage, this one by a *psychoanalytic* critic.

11. *The* Oedipus Rex *is a tragedy of fate: its tragic effect depends on the conflict between the all-powerful will of the*

gods and the vain efforts of human beings threatened with disaster; resignation to the divine will, and the perception of one's own impotence is the lesson which the deeply moved spectator is supposed to learn from the tragedy. Modern authors have therefore sought to achieve a similar tragic effect by expressing the same conflict in stories of their own invention. But the playgoers have looked on unmoved . . . The modern tragedies of destiny have failed of their effect. If the Oedipus Rex *is capable of moving a modern reader or play-goer no less powerfully than it moved the contemporary Greeks, the only possible explanation is that the effect of the Greek tragedy does not depend upon the conflict between fate and human will, but upon the peculiar nature of the material by which this conflict is revealed. There must be a voice within us which is prepared to acknowledge the compelling power of fate in the* Oedipus, *. . . this [Oedipus's] fate moves us only because it might have been our own, because the oracle laid upon us before our birth the very curse which rested upon him. It may be that we were all destined to direct our first sexual impulses toward our mothers and our first impulses of hatred and violence toward our fathers; our dreams convince us that we were.*

> "The Interpretation of Dreams," in *The Basic Writings of Sigmund Freud*, Random House, 1938.

At this point we recall that Jocasta has spoken of such dreams (p. 67B). And Freud, in accordance with the theory of psychoanalysis which he founded, goes on to view a work of art as a dream, a fantasy:

12. *King Oedipus, who slew his father Laius and wedded his mother Jocasta, is nothing more or less than a wish-fulfillment —the fulfillment of the wish of our childhood. But we, more fortunate than he, in so far as we have not become psycho-neurotics, have since our childhood succeeded in withdrawing our sexual impulses from our mothers and in forgetting our*

jealousy of our fathers. We recoil from the person for whom this primitive wish of our childhood has been fulfilled with all the force of the repression which these wishes have undergone in our minds since childhood. As the poet brings the guilt of Oedipus to light by his investigation, he forces us to become aware of our own inner selves, in which the same impulses are still extant, even though they are suppressed . . . Like Oedipus, we live in ignorance of the desires that offend morality, the desires that nature has forced upon us and, after their unveiling, we may well prefer to avert our gaze from the scenes of our childhood.

> "The Interpretation of Dreams,"
> Sigmund Freud.

Now let us examine a rebuttal of the Freudian view.

13. *This famous passage is, of course, a landmark in the history of modern thought, and it is a token of the vitality of Greek literature that in these sentences one of the most bitterly contested and influential concepts of the modern mind takes the form of an attempt to solve a critical problem raised by the Sophoclean play. But quite apart from the value (or lack of it) of Freud's theory of the Oedipus complex (which he here announced for the first time), the solution he proposes to the critical problem raised by calling the play a "tragedy of fate" cannot be accepted. When he says that Oedipus' fate affects us because "it might have been our own" he has put his finger on an essential aspect of the tragedy, the universality of the theme, which of course extends far beyond the particular appeal which Freud himself here expounds. But the universal appeal of the theme, whether understood in psychoanalytical or other terms, does not explain the dramatic excitement generated by the tragedy. No amount of symbolic richness—conscious, subconscious, or unconscious— will create dramatic excitement in a play which does not possess the essential prerequisites of human free will and responsibility. The tragedy must be self-sufficient: that is, the*

catastrophe must be the result of the free decision and action (or inaction) of the tragic protagonist.

The problem, stated in Freud's terms (and he only states in extreme form what many others imply or assume), is obviously insoluble. If the Oedipus Tyrannus *is a "tragedy of fate," the hero's will is not free, and the dramatic efficiency of the play is limited by that fact. The problem is insoluble; but luckily the problem does not exist to start with. For in the play which Sophocles wrote, the hero's will is absolutely free and he is fully responsible for the catastrophe.*

Oedipus at Thebes, Bernard Knox.

14. *Professor Waldock, who writes with refreshing good sense about the plays and their problems, objects to the notion that great plays must contain profound truths, or even "mean something"; to him* Œdipus Rex *is simply a wonderful story, rather than a universal situation. The whole uncertainty about the "meaning" of these plays would seem to indicate that their greatness does not depend on any specific meaning. Yet Sophocles was manifestly a thoughtful writer, concerned with major issues of human conduct and human destiny. Almost all readers feel that his plays positively do "mean something" —that he was expressing, however obliquely, some "philosophy of life." And almost all commentators agree on certain qualities that are clues to his thought, notably his irony and his refusal to declare himself in so many words. In our own world these might imply a devotion to art for art's sake. In the Greek world they imply a measure of philosophical skepticism. Sophocles was at least saying that the ways of deity are mysterious, and often painfully so.*

The Spirit of Tragedy, Herbert J. Muller, Washington Square Press, 1965.

15. *[Oedipus's] . . . humiliation is a lesson both to others and to him. Democritus's words, "the foolish learn modesty in misfortune," may be applied to Oedipus, who has indeed*

*been foolish in his mistakes and illusions and has been taught
modesty through suffering.*

> *Sophoclean Tragedy,* C. M. Bowra,
> Oxford University Press, 1944.

16. *It has been suggested by Professor Ellis-Fermor that the
catharsis of plays like . . . [Oedipus] . . . lies in the perfection
of their form, which, by implication, represents the forces of
righteousness and beneficence . . . the Greek believed, as if by
instinct, that the universe was not chaotic and "irrational"
but was based on a logos, obeyed Law. . . . Every detail in the
Tyrannus is contrived in order to enforce Sophocles' faith in
this underlying logos; that is the reason why it is true to say
that the perfection of its form implies a world order. Whether
or not it is beneficent, Sophocles does not say.*

> *Greek Tragedy,* H. D. F. Kitto,
> Doubleday and Co., 1954.

17. *Thebes suffers because of Oedipus, and Oedipus suffers
because of Laius. Since the play is based on the concept of
oneness, the associated concepts of transferred guilt and
inherited guilt are fundamental elements of this tragedy.
. . . Life is an inheritance which we receive with all its liabil-
ities. . . . Guilt, if incurred by a progenitor, clings to our
inherited life. . . .*

> *Renunciation as a Tragic Focus,*
> Eugene H. Falk, University of Min-
> nesota Press, 1954.

Here, surely, we have a great variety of views, few of them
exclusive of the others. What is your reaction to the fact that
at least one professor enjoys *Oedipus* as "simply a wonderful
story"? Do you find Oedipus's resignation, his acceptance of
inherited guilt, compatible with *your* notions of free will?

We have reserved the last comment in our "critical sampler"
for the concluding passage in the detailed study of *Oedipus*
written by our translator—who is also the writer of, and the
commentator in, a series of four films on *Oedipus the King:*

18. *Oedipus is symbolic of all human achievement: his hard-won magnificence, unlike the everlasting magnificence of the divine, cannot last, and while it lives, shines all the more brilliant against the somber background of its impermanency. Sophocles' tragedy presents us with a terrible affirmation of man's subordinate position in the universe, and at the same time with a heroic vision of man's victory in defeat. Man is not equated to the gods, but man at his greatest, as in Oedipus, is capable of something which the gods, by definition, cannot experience; the proud tragic view of Sophocles sees in the fragility and inevitable defeat of human greatness the possibility of a purely human heroism to which the gods can never attain, for the condition of their existence is everlasting victory.*

Oedipus at Thebes, Bernard Knox.

19. *Now, why is it that today, when no man alive believes in Apollo or worries about the Delphic oracle, lovers of literature still find themselves involved in Oedipus's problems and his personality? Obviously Sophocles deals here with a universal situation that transcends the interests and circumstances of fifth-century B.C. Athens. Oedipus is a symbolic figure for all mankind.*

Most significant to us, perhaps, is Oedipus's noble assumption of full responsibility for his own past. In an obvious sense, his troubles have been caused by Laius and Jocasta's blind way of handling their problems, by the shepherd's failure to obey orders, by Polybus and Merope's unwillingness to tell him the truth. Yet Oedipus recognizes that each man is an embodiment of his own heritage and must accept the consequences of his own personality, even if he did not create that personality all by himself.

Secondly, we all operate, most of the time, in partial ignorance of the full situation. We are all, at any time, liable to discover that we have oversimplified. We are all in danger of assuming that because we defeated one Sphinx, we can defeat all Sphinxes. Oedipus appalls us, and we identify with him because he illustrates the ridiculously conflicting demands

*made on man. He must act as if he knows what he is doing
when he cannot possibly be sure of ultimate causes or effects.*

*Thirdly, like Oedipus, we all suffer some difficulties with
the older generation, with authority figures. It is inevitable—
as children grow up and test out their own powers—that there
be some conflict of interest with their parents. Oedipus's fears
that he may hurt his parents find an echo in everyone who
wants to be strong and independent, yet sensitive and fair.*

*Fourthly, we all identify with Oedipus's passionate drive to
know more about his own nature. To what extent is our life
determined by heredity, environment, body chemistry, instinct,
and the ultimate forces in the universe? To what extent can
anybody enjoy free will? To what extent are we too the children of Chance (p. 79M)? Puny in the reaches of time and
space, situated vaguely midway between the atoms and the
stars, like Oedipus, we want to understand the relationship
between our finite world and the infinity beyond. We can
accept Apollo and Delphi as symbols of the Ultimate Reality
and Oedipus as symbolizing man's drive to know his part in
the scheme of things.*

"Character Analysis," *Oedipus the
King,* Walter James Miller, Washington Square Press, 1967.

20. *Even among psychoanalysts, the so-called "Oedipus complex" is a controversial question. It might be valuable here,
in connection with the play that gave the "complex" its name,
to review three hypotheses about the nature of the "Oedipal
situation."*

*Here is a summary of Freud's position as given in a stan-
dard text,* Childhood and Adolescence, *by L. J. Stone and
Joseph Church:*

The term "Oedipus complex" comes from the Greek
myth of King Oedipus, who unwittingly, but in fulfillment of an old prophecy, killed his father and married
his mother. Analogously, the small boy is seen as falling
in love with his mother and turning against his father as
a rival for her affections. Naturally, these strivings are

opposed by the realities of the situation, by the child's
sense of danger in competing with an all-powerful father,
and by contradictory impulses of affection for the father
and resentment (as when she disciplines him) against the
mother. The normal outcome of this (in Freud's view)
universal conflict *of opposing forces is to align and iden-*
tify oneself with the father, submerging (i.e., repressing)
the unacceptable wishes. . . . In regard to turning against
the parents, although adults were long loath to accept the
fact, children are ambivalent *about their parents; that*
is, they blend or alternate hostility with affection. It like-
wise seems to be true, as Freud proposed, that children
feel guilty about their anger and conceal or deny it.

Erich Fromm, *regarded as one of our foremost living*
psychoanalysts, claims that the Oedipus "myth has to be
understood not as a symbol of the incestuous tie between
mother and son, but as the rebellion of the son against the
authority of the father in the patriarchal family; and that the
marriage of Oedipus and Jocasta is only a secondary element,
only one of the symbols of the son's victory, who takes over
his father's place and with it all his privileges."

Another distinguished psychoanalyst, Harry Stack Sullivan,
also sees the "Oedipal situation" differently from Freud. Ac-
cording to Patrick Mullahy, in his Oedipus: Myth and Complex:

   Sullivan attaches fundamental importance to the role
   of the parents, especially the mother or her surrogate in
   infancy and childhood. But this role is not a sexual one,
   even in the wide sense in which Freud conceives sexual-
   ity. The feeling of familiarity which a parent has toward
   his or her child of the same sex is said to lead to an
   authoritarian attitude, which, of course, produces resent-
   ment and hostility in the child. On the other hand, be-
   cause of the difference in sex, leading to a sense of
   strangeness, the parent treats his or her child of the op-
   posite sex with more consideration. Why? In the first
   case, the parent thinks that he is justified in dictating to
   someone who seems to be like himself, while in the latter

*case the feeling of strangeness deprives him of the notion
that he is peculiarly fitted to run the child's life. Hence
parents tend to treat their children of the opposite sex,
so to speak, "with kid gloves." In this case, the freedom
or relative freedom from pressure by the parent of the
other sex results, at least often, in a feeling of greater
affection and attraction by the child for him.*

Ibid., Walter James Miller.

yours are hardest to bear for their owners—and justly so.

OEDIPUS

Get out, will you? Out!

CREON

I am going. I found you ignorant—but these men think I am right.

[*Exit Creon to side.*]

CHORUS

[*To Jocasta*]

Lady, why don't you get him into the house quickly?

JOCASTA

I will—when I have found out what happened here.

CHORUS

There was some ignorant talk based on hearsay and some hurt caused by injustice.

47

JOCASTA

On both sides?

CHORUS

Yes.

JOCASTA

And what did they say?

CHORUS

Enough, that is enough, it seems to me. I speak in the interests of the whole country. Let this matter lie where they left it.

OEDIPUS

You see where your good intentions have brought you. This is the result of turning aside and blunting the edge of my anger.

CHORUS

My king, I said it before, more than once—listen to me. I would be exposed as a madman, useless, brainless, if I were to turn my back on you. You found Thebes laboring in a sea of trouble, you righted her and set her on a fair course. All I wish now is that you should guide us as well as you did then.

JOCASTA

In God's name, explain to me, my lord—what was it made you so angry?

OEDIPUS

I will tell you. I have more respect for you than for these people here. Creon and his conspiracy against me, that's what made me angry.

JOCASTA

Tell me clearly, what was the quarrel between you?

OEDIPUS

He says that *I* am the murderer of Laius.

JOCASTA

On what evidence? His own knowledge, or hearsay?

OEDIPUS

Oh, he keeps his own lips clear of responsibility
—he sent a swindling prophet in to speak for him.

JOCASTA

A prophet? In that case, rid your mind of your
fear, and listen to me. I can teach you something.
There is no human being born that is endowed with
prophetic power. I can prove it to you—and in a
few words.

A prophecy came to Laius once—I won't say
from Apollo himself, but from his priests. It said
that Laius was fated to die by the hand of his son,
a son to be born to him and to me. Well, Laius, so the
story goes, was killed by foreign robbers at a place
where three highways meet. As for the son—three
days after his birth Laius fastened his ankles together and had him cast away on the pathless
mountains.

So, in this case, Apollo did not make the son kill
his father or Laius die by his own son's hand, as he
had feared. Yet these were the definite statements of
the prophetic voices. Don't pay any attention to
prophecies. If God seeks or needs anything, he will
easily make it clear to us himself.

OEDIPUS

Jocasta, something I heard you say has disturbed me to the soul, unhinged my mind.

JOCASTA

What do you mean? What was it that alarmed you so?

OEDIPUS

I thought I heard you say that Laius was killed at a place where three highways meet.

JOCASTA

Yes, that's what the story was—and still is.

OEDIPUS

Where is the place where this thing happened?

JOCASTA

The country is called Phocis: two roads, one from Delphi and one from Daulia, come together and form one.

51

OEDIPUS

When did it happen? How long ago?

JOCASTA

We heard the news here in Thebes just before you appeared and became King.

OEDIPUS

O God, what have you planned to do to me?

JOCASTA

What is it, Oedipus, which haunts your spirit so?

OEDIPUS

No questions, not yet. Laius—tell me what he looked like, how old he was.

JOCASTA

He was a big man—his hair had just begun to turn white. And he had more or less the same build as you.

52

OEDIPUS

O God! I think I have just called down on myself a dreadful curse—not knowing what I did.

JOCASTA

What do you mean? To look at you makes me
shudder, my lord.

OEDIPUS

I am dreadfully afraid the blind prophet could
see. But tell me one more thing that will throw
light on this.

JOCASTA

I am afraid. But ask your question; I will answer
if I can.

OEDIPUS

Was Laius poorly attended, or did he have a
big bodyguard, like a king?

JOCASTA

There were five men in his party. One of them
was a herald. And there was one wagon—Laius was
riding in it.

OEDIPUS

Oh, it is all clear as daylight now. Who was it told you all this at the time?

JOCASTA

A slave from the royal household. He was the only one who came back.

OEDIPUS

Is he by any chance in the palace now?

JOCASTA

No, he is not. When he came back and saw you ruling in place of Laius, he seized my hand and begged me to send him to work in the country, to the pastures, to the flocks, as far away as I could —out of sight of Thebes. And I sent him. Though he was a slave he deserved this favor from me—and much more.

OEDIPUS

Can I get him back here, in haste?

54

JOCASTA

It can be done. But why are you so intent on this?

OEDIPUS

I am afraid, Jocasta, that I have said too much— that's why I want to see this man.

JOCASTA

Well, he shall come. But I have a right, it seems to me, to know what it is that torments you so.

OEDIPUS

So you shall. Since I am so full of dreadful expectation, I shall hold nothing back from you. Who else should I speak to, who means more to me than you, in this time of trouble?

My father was Polybus, a Dorian, and my mother Merope, of Corinth. I was regarded as the greatest man in that city until something happened to me quite by chance, a strange thing, but not worth all the attention I paid it. A man at the banquet table, who had had too much to drink, told me, over his wine, that I was not the true son of my father. I was furious, but, hard though it was, I con-

55

trolled my feelings, for that day at least. On the next day I went to my parents and questioned them. They were enraged against the man who had so taunted me. So I took comfort from their attitude, but still the thing tormented me—for the story spread far and wide. Without telling my parents, I set off on a journey to the oracle of Apollo, at Delphi. Apollo sent me away with my question unanswered but he foretold a dreadful, calamitous future for me—to lie with my mother and beget children men's eyes would not bear the sight of—and to be the killer of the father that gave me life.

When I heard that, I ran away. From that point on I measured the distance to the land of Corinth by the stars. I was running to a place where I would never see that shameful prophecy come true. On my way I came to the place in which you say this king, Laius, met his death.

I will tell you the truth, all of it. As I journeyed on I came near to this triple crossroad and there I was met by a herald and a man riding on a horse-drawn wagon, just as you described it. The driver, and the old man himself, tried to push me off the road. In anger I struck the driver as he tried to crowd me off. When the old man saw me coming past the wheels he aimed at my head with a two-pronged goad, and hit me. I paid him back in full, with interest: in no time at all he was hit by the stick I held in my hand and rolled backwards from the center of the wagon. I killed the whole lot of them.

Now, if this stranger had anything to do with Laius—is there a more unhappy man alive than I? Who could be more hateful to the gods than I am? No foreigner or citizen may take me into his house, no one can talk to me—everyone must expel me from his home. And the man who called down these curses on me was I myself, no one else. With these hands that killed him I defile the dead man's marriage bed. How can I deny that I am vile, utterly unclean? I must be banished from Thebes, and then I may not even see my own parents or set foot on my own fatherland—or else I am doomed to marry my own mother and kill my father Polybus, who brought me up and gave me life. I am the victim of some harsh divinity; what other explanation can there be?

Let it not happen, not that, I beg you, holy majesty of God, may I never see that day! May I disappear from among men without trace before I see such a stain of misfortune come upon me!

57

CHORUS LEADER

My lord, this makes us tremble. But do not despair—you have still to hear the story from the eyewitness.

OEDIPUS

That's right. That's my hope now, such as it is—to wait for the shepherd.

JOCASTA

Why all this urgency about his coming?

OEDIPUS

I'll tell you. If it turns out that he tells the same story as you—then I, at least, will be cleared of responsibility.

JOCASTA

What was so important in what you heard from me?

OEDIPUS

You said his story was that *several* robbers killed Laius. Well, if he speaks of the same number as you—then I am not the killer. For one could never be equal to many. But if he speaks of one man alone—then clearly the balance tips towards me as the killer.

JOCASTA

You can be sure that his account was made public just as I told it to you; he cannot go back on it, the whole city heard it, not I alone. But, my lord, even if he should depart from his former account in some particular, he still would never make the death of Laius what it was supposed to be—for Apollo said clearly that Laius was to be killed by my son. But that poor infant never killed Laius; it met its own death first. So much for prophecy. For all it can say, I would not, from now on, so much as look to right or left.

OEDIPUS

Yes, I agree. But all the same, that shepherd— send someone to fetch him. Do it at once.

JOCASTA

I shall send immediately. And now let us go in. I would not do anything except what pleases you.

[*Exeunt Oedipus and Jocasta through doors.*]

59

CHORUS

[*Chanting in unison*]

May Destiny be with me always;
Let me observe reverence and purity
In word and deed.
Laws that stand above have been established—
Born in the upper air on high;
Their only father is heaven;
No mortal nature, no man gave them birth.
They never forget, or sleep.
In them God is great, and He does not grow
   old.

The despot is the child of violent pride,
Pride that vainly stuffs itself
With food unseasonable, unfit,
Climbs to the highest rim
And then plunges sheer down into defeat
Where its feet are of no use.
Yet I pray to God to spare that vigor
Which benefits the state.
God is my protector, on Him I shall never cease
   to call.

The man who goes his way
Overbearing in word and deed,
Who fears no justice,
Honors no temples of the gods—
May an evil destiny seize him
And punish his ill-starred pride.
How shall such a man defend his life
Against God's arrows?
If such deeds as this are honored,
Why should we join the sacred dance and wor-
    ship?

I shall go no more in reverence to Delphi,
The holy center of the earth,
Nor to any temple in the world,
Unless these prophecies come true,
For all men to point at in wonder.
O Zeus, King of heaven, ruler of all,
If you deserve this name,
Do not let your everlasting power be deceived,
Do not forget.
The old prophecies about Laius are failing,
Men reject them now.
Apollo is without honor everywhere.
The gods are defeated.

[*Enter Jocasta, with branches of olive.*]

JOCASTA

[*To chorus*]

Lords of Thebes, it occurred to me to come to the temples of the gods bearing in my hands these branches and offerings of incense. For Oedipus is distracted with sorrows of all kinds. He does not act like a man in control of his reason, judging the present by the past—he is at the mercy of anyone who speaks to him, especially one who speaks of terrors. I have given him advice, but it does no good. [*Facing the altar*] So I come to you, Lord Apollo, for you are closest to hand. I come in supplication with these emblems of prayer. Deliver us, make us free and clear of defilement. We are all afraid, like passengers on a ship who see their pilot crazed with fear.

[*Enter from side Corinthian messenger.*]

CORINTHIAN MESSENGER

[*To chorus*]

Strangers, can one of you tell me—where is the palace of King Oedipus? Better still, if you know, where is the king himself?

62

CHORUS LEADER

This is his palace, and he is inside, stranger. This lady is his queen, his wife and mother of his children.

CORINTHIAN MESSENGER

Greetings to the noble wife of Oedipus! May you and all your family be blessed forever.

JOCASTA

The same blessings on you, stranger, for your kind words. But tell us what you want. Why have you come? Have you some news for us?

CORINTHIAN MESSENGER

Good news for your house and your husband, lady.

JOCASTA

What news? Who sent you?

CORINTHIAN MESSENGER

I come from Corinth. My message will bring you joy—no doubt of that—but sorrow, too.

63

JOCASTA

What is it? How can it work both ways?

CORINTHIAN MESSENGER

The people of Corinth will make Oedipus their king, so I heard there.

JOCASTA

What? Is old Polybus no longer on the throne?

CORINTHIAN MESSENGER

No. He is dead and in his grave.

JOCASTA

What did you say? Polybus is dead? Dead?

CORINTHIAN MESSENGER

Condemn me to death if I am not telling the truth.

JOCASTA

[*To servant*]

You there, go in quickly and tell your master.

O prophecies of the gods, where are you now?

64

Polybus was the man Oedipus feared he might kill
—and so avoided him all this time. And now he's
dead—a natural death, and not by the hand of Oedipus.

[*Enter Oedipus, from doors.*]

OEDIPUS

Jocasta, why did you send for me to come out
here?

JOCASTA

Listen to what this man says, and see what has
become of the holy prophecies of the gods.

OEDIPUS

Who is he? What does he have to say to me?

JOCASTA

He's from Corinth. He came to tell you that
your father Polybus is dead and gone.

OEDIPUS

Is this true? Tell me yourself.

CORINTHIAN MESSENGER

If that's what you want to hear first, here it is, a plain statement: Polybus is dead and gone.

OEDIPUS

How? Killed by a traitor, or wasted by disease?

CORINTHIAN MESSENGER

He was old. It did not take much to put him to sleep.

OEDIPUS

By disease, then—that's how he died?

CORINTHIAN MESSENGER

Yes, that, and the length of years he had lived.

OEDIPUS

So! Why then, Jocasta, should we study Apollo's oracle, or gaze at the birds screaming over our heads —those prophets who announced that I would kill my father? He's dead, buried, below ground. And here I am in Thebes—I did not put hand to sword.

Perhaps he died from longing to see me again.
66

That way, it could be said that I was the cause of his death. But there he lies, dead, taking with him all these prophecies I feared—they are worth nothing!

JOCASTA

Is that not what I told you?

OEDIPUS

It is. But I was led astray by fear.

JOCASTA

Now rid your heart of fear forever.

OEDIPUS

No, I must still fear—and who would not?—a marriage with my mother.

JOCASTA

Fear? Why should man fear? His life is governed by the operations of chance. Nothing can be clearly foreseen. The best way to live is by hit and miss, as best you can. Don't be afraid that you may marry your mother. Many a man before you, in dreams, has shared his mother's bed. But to live at ease one must attach no importance to such things.

67

OEDIPUS

All that you have said would be fine—if my mother were not still alive. But she is, and no matter how good a case you make, I am still a prey to fear.

JOCASTA

But your father's death—that much at least is a great blessing.

OEDIPUS

Yes, I see that. But my mother, as long as she is alive, fills me with fear.

CORINTHIAN MESSENGER

Who is this woman that inspires such fear in you?

OEDIPUS

Merope, old man, the wife of Polybus.

CORINTHIAN MESSENGER

And what is there about her which frightens you?

68

OEDIPUS

A dreadful prophecy sent by the gods.

CORINTHIAN MESSENGER

Can you tell me what it is? Or is it forbidden for others to know?

OEDIPUS

Yes, I can tell you. Apollo once announced that I am destined to mate with my mother, and shed my father's blood with my own hand. That is why for so many years I have lived far away from Corinth. It has turned out well—but still, there's nothing sweeter than the sight of one's parents.

CORINTHIAN MESSENGER

Is that it? It was in fear of this that you banished yourself from Corinth?

OEDIPUS

Yes. I did not want to be my father's murderer.

CORINTHIAN MESSENGER

My lord, I do not know why I have not already

released you from that fear. I came here to bring you good news.

OEDIPUS

If you can do that, you will be handsomely rewarded.

CORINTHIAN MESSENGER

Yes, that was why I came, to bring you home to Corinth, and be rewarded for it.

OEDIPUS

I will never go to the city where my parents live.

CORINTHIAN MESSENGER

My son, it is clear that you don't know what you are doing.

OEDIPUS

What do you mean, old man? In God's name, explain yourself.

70

CORINTHIAN MESSENGER

You don't know what you are doing, if you are afraid to come home because of *them*.

OEDIPUS

I am afraid that Apollo's prophecy may come true.

CORINTHIAN MESSENGER

That you will be stained with guilt through your parents?

OEDIPUS

Yes, that's it, old man, that's the fear which pursues me always.

CORINTHIAN MESSENGER

In reality, you have nothing to fear.

OEDIPUS

Nothing? How, if I am the son of Polybus and Merope?

71

CORINTHIAN MESSENGER

Because Polybus was not related to you in any way.

OEDIPUS

What do you mean? Was Polybus not my father?

CORINTHIAN MESSENGER

No more than I am—he was as much your father as I.

OEDIPUS

How can my father be on the same level as you who are nothing to me?

CORINTHIAN MESSENGER

Because he was no more your father than I am.

OEDIPUS

Then why did he call me his son?

CORINTHIAN MESSENGER

He took you from my hands—I gave you to him.

72

OEDIPUS

Took me from your hands? Then how could
he love me so much?

CORINTHIAN MESSENGER

He had been childless, that was why he loved
you.

OEDIPUS

You gave me to him? Did you . . . buy me? or
find me somewhere?

CORINTHIAN MESSENGER

I found you in the shady valleys of Mount
Cithaeron.

OEDIPUS

What were you doing there?

CORINTHIAN MESSENGER

Watching over my flocks on the mountainside.

OEDIPUS

A shepherd, were you? A wandering day
laborer?

73

CORINTHIAN MESSENGER

Yes, but at that moment I was your savior.

OEDIPUS

When you picked me up, was I in pain?

CORINTHIAN MESSENGER

Your ankles would bear witness on that point.

OEDIPUS

Oh, why do you speak of that old affliction?

CORINTHIAN MESSENGER

You had your ankles pinned together, and I freed you.

OEDIPUS

It is a dreadful mark of shame I have borne since childhood.

CORINTHIAN MESSENGER

From that misfortune comes the name which you still bear. *

---

* His name, Oedipus, means, in Greek, "swollen foot."

OEDIPUS

In God's name, who did it? My mother, or my father? Speak.

CORINTHIAN MESSENGER

I don't know. The one who gave you to me is the man to ask, not me.

OEDIPUS

You got me from someone else—you did not find me yourself?

CORINTHIAN MESSENGER

No. Another shepherd gave you to me.

OEDIPUS

Who was he? Do you know? Could you describe him?

CORINTHIAN MESSENGER

I think he belonged to the household of Laius.

OEDIPUS

You mean the man who was once king of this country?

CORINTHIAN MESSENGER

Yes. He was one of the shepherds of Laius.

OEDIPUS

Is he still alive? Can I talk to him?

CORINTHIAN MESSENGER

[*To chorus*]

You people who live here would know that better than I.

OEDIPUS

[*To chorus*]

Is there any one of you people here who knows this shepherd he mentioned? Has anyone seen him in the fields, or here in Thebes?

CHORUS LEADER

I think it is the same man from the fields you wanted to see before. But the queen here, Jocasta, could tell you that.

OEDIPUS

Jocasta, do you remember the man we sent for just now? Is *that* the man he is talking about?

76

JOCASTA

Why ask who he means? Don't pay any attention to him. Don't even think about what he said —it makes no sense.

OEDIPUS

What? With a clue like this? Give up the search? Fail to solve the mystery of my birth? Never!

JOCASTA

In God's name, if you place any value on your life, don't pursue the search. It is enough that *I* am sick to death.

OEDIPUS

You have nothing to be afraid of. Even if my mother turns out to be a slave, and I a slave for three generations back, *your* noble birth will not be called in question.

JOCASTA

Take my advice, I beg you—do not go on with it.

OEDIPUS

Nothing will move me. I *will* find out the whole truth.

77

JOCASTA

It is good advice I am giving you—I am thinking of you.

OEDIPUS

That "good advice" of yours is trying my patience.

JOCASTA

Ill-fated man. May you never find out who you are!

OEDIPUS

[*To attendants*]

One of you go and get that shepherd, bring him here. We will leave *her* to pride herself on her royal birth.

JOCASTA

Unfortunate! That is the only name I can call you by now. I shall not call your name again—ever!

[*Exit Jocasta to palace.*]

[*A long silence.*]

78

CHORUS

Why has the queen gone, Oedipus, why has she rushed away in such wild grief? I am afraid that from this silence evil will burst out.

OEDIPUS

Burst out what will! I shall know my origin, mean though it be. Jocasta perhaps—she is proud, *like* a woman—feels shame at the low circumstances of my birth. But I count myself the son of Good Chance, the giver of success—I shall not be dishonored. Chance is my mother. My brothers are the months which have made me sometimes small and sometimes great. Such is my lineage and I shall not betray it. I will not give up the search for the truth about my birth.

[*Exit Oedipus to palace.*]

CHORUS

[*Chanting in unison*]

If I am a true prophet
And see clear in my mind,
Tomorrow at the full moon
Oedipus will honor Mount Cithaeron
As his nurse and mother.

Mount Cithaeron—our king's Theban birthplace!
We shall celebrate it in dance and song—
A place loved by our king.
Lord Apollo, may this find favor in your sight.

Who was it, Oedipus my son, who bore you?
Which of the nymphs that live so long
Was the bride of Pan the mountain god?
Was your mother the bride of Apollo himself?
He loves the upland pastures.
Or was Hermes your father?
Perhaps Dionysus who lives on the mountain
    peaks
Received you as a welcome gift
From one of the nymphs of Helicon,
His companions in sport.

[*Enter from side the shepherd, accompanied by
two guards.*]

[*Enter Oedipus, from doors.*]

OEDIPUS

I never met the man, but, if I may make a guess,
I think this man I see is the shepherd we have been
looking for all this time. His age corresponds to that
of the Corinthian here, and, in any case, the men
bringing him are my servants, I recognize them.

80

[*To chorus leader*] You have seen the shepherd before, you should know better than I.

CHORUS LEADER

Yes, I recognize him. He was in the household of Laius—a devoted servant, and a shepherd.

OEDIPUS

I question you first—you, the stranger from Corinth. Is this the man you spoke of?

CORINTHIAN MESSENGER

This is the man.

OEDIPUS

[*To shepherd*]

You, old man, come here. Look me in the face. Answer my questions. Were you a servant of Laius once?

SHEPHERD

I was. A slave. Not bought, though. I was born and reared in the palace.

OEDIPUS

What was your work? How did you earn your living?

SHEPHERD

For most of my life I have followed where the sheep flocks went.

OEDIPUS

And where did you graze your sheep most of the time?

SHEPHERD

Well, there was Mount Cithaeron, and all the country round it.

OEDIPUS

Do you know this man here? Did you ever see him before?

SHEPHERD

Which man do you mean? What would he be doing there?

82

OEDIPUS

This one, here. Did you ever come across him?

SHEPHERD

I can't say, right away. Give me time. I don't remember.

CORINTHIAN MESSENGER

No wonder he doesn't remember, master. He forgets, but I'll remind him, and make it clear. I am sure he knows very well how the two of us grazed our flocks on Cithaeron—he had two and I only one—we were together three whole summers, from spring until the rising of Arcturus in the fall. When winter came I used to herd my sheep back to their winter huts, and he took his back to the farms belonging to Laius. Do you remember any of this? Isn't that what happened?

SHEPHERD

What you say is true, but it was a long time ago.

CORINTHIAN MESSENGER

Well, then, tell me this. Do you remember giving me a child, a boy, for me to bring up as my own?

SHEPHERD

What are you talking about? Why do you ask that question?

CORINTHIAN MESSENGER

Oedipus here, my good man, Oedipus and that child are one and the same.

SHEPHERD

Damn you! Shut your mouth. Keep quiet!

OEDIPUS

Old man, don't you correct *him*. It is you and your tongue that need correction.

SHEPHERD

What have I done wrong, noble master?

OEDIPUS

You refuse to answer his question about the child.

SHEPHERD

That's because he does not know what he's talking about—he is just wasting your time.

OEDIPUS

If you won't speak willingly, we shall see if pain
can make you speak.

[*The guards seize the shepherd.*]

SHEPHERD

In God's name, don't! Don't torture me. I am
an old man.

OEDIPUS

One of you twist his arms behind his back,
quickly!

SHEPHERD

Oh, God, what for? What more do you want to
know?

OEDIPUS

Did you give him the child he asked about?

SHEPHERD

Yes, I did. And I wish I had died that day.

OEDIPUS

You will die now, if you don't give an honest
answer.

85

SHEPHERD

And if I speak, I shall be even worse off.

OEDIPUS

[*To guards*]

What? More delay?

SHEPHERD

No! No! I said it before—I gave him the child.

OEDIPUS

Where did *you* get it? Was it yours? Or did it belong to someone else?

SHEPHERD

It wasn't mine. Someone gave it to me.

OEDIPUS

Which of these Thebans here? From whose house did it come?

SHEPHERD

In God's name, master, don't ask any more questions.

86

OEDIPUS

You are a dead man if I have to ask you again.

SHEPHERD

It was a child born in the house of Laius.

OEDIPUS

Was it a slave? Or a member of the royal family?

SHEPHERD

Oh, God, here comes the dreadful truth. And I must speak.

OEDIPUS

And I must hear it. But hear it I will.

SHEPHERD

It was the son of Laius, so I was told. But the lady inside there, your wife, she is the one to tell you.

OEDIPUS

Did *she* give it to you?

87

SHEPHERD

Yes, my lord, she did.

OEDIPUS

For what purpose?

SHEPHERD

To destroy it.

OEDIPUS

Her own child?

SHEPHERD

She was afraid of dreadful prophecies.

OEDIPUS

What were they?

SHEPHERD

The child would kill its parents, that was the story.

88

OEDIPUS

Then why did you give it to this old man here?

SHEPHERD

In pity, master. I thought he would take it away to a foreign country—to the place he came from. If you are the man he says you are, you were born the most unfortunate of men.

OEDIPUS

O God! It has all come true. Light, let this be the last time I see you. I stand revealed—born in shame, married in shame, an unnatural murderer.

[*Exit Oedipus into palace.*]

[*Exeunt others at sides.*]

CHORUS

O generations of mortal men,
I add up the total of your lives
And find it equal to nothing.
What man wins more happiness
Than a mere appearance which quickly fades
   away?
With your example before me,

Your life, your destiny, miserable Oedipus,
      I call no man happy.

Oedipus outranged all others
And won complete prosperity and happiness.
He destroyed the Sphinx, that maiden
With curved claws and riddling songs,
And rose up like a towered wall against death—
Oedipus, savior of our city.
From that time on you were called King,
You were honored above all men,
Ruling over great Thebes.

And now—is there a man whose story is more
    pitiful?
His life is lived in merciless calamity and pain—
A complete reversal from his happy state.
O Oedipus, famous king,
You whom the same great harbor sheltered
As child and father both,
How could the furrows which your father
    plowed
Bear *you* in silence for so long?

Time, which sees all things, has found you out;
It sits in judgment on the unnatural marriage
Which was both begetter and begot.

O son of Laius,
I wish I had never seen you.
I weep, like a man wailing for the dead.
        This is the truth:
You returned me to life once
And now you have closed my eyes in darkness.

[*Enter, from the palace, a messenger.*]

MESSENGER

Citizens of Thebes, you who are most honored in this city! What dreadful things you will see and hear! What a cry of sorrow you will raise, if, as true Thebans, you have any feeling for the royal house. Not even the great rivers of Ister and Phasis could wash this house clean of the horrors it hides within. And it will soon expose them to the light of day—horrors deliberately willed, not involuntary. Those calamities we inflict on ourselves are those which cause the most pain.

CHORUS LEADER

The horrors we knew about before were burden enough. What other dreadful news do you bring?

MESSENGER

Here is the thing quickest for me to say and you to hear. Jocasta, our queen, is dead.

CHORUS LEADER

Poor lady. From what cause?

MESSENGER

By her own hand. You are spared the worst of what has happened—you were not there to see it. But as far as my memory serves, you shall hear the full story of that unhappy woman's sufferings.

She came in through the door in a fury of passion and rushed straight towards her marriage bed, tearing at her hair with both hands. Into her bedroom she went, and slammed the doors behind her. She was calling the name of Laius, so long dead, remembering the child she bore to him so long ago— the child by whose hand Laius was to die, and leave her, its mother, to bear monstrous children to her own son. She wailed in mourning for her marriage, in which she had borne double offspring, a husband from her husband and children from her child. And after that—but I do not know exactly how she died. For Oedipus came bursting in, shouting, and so we could not watch Jocasta's suffering to the end; all of us looked at him as he ran to and fro. He rushed from one of us to the other, asking us to give him a sword, to tell him where he could find his wife—no, not his wife, but his mother, his mother and the mother of his children.

It must have been some supernatural being that showed the raving man where she was; it was not one of us. As if led by a guide he threw himself against the doors of her room with a terrible cry; he bent the bolts out of their sockets, and so forced his way into the room. And there we saw Jocasta, hanging, her neck caught in a swinging noose of rope. When Oedipus saw her he gave a deep dreadful cry of sorrow and loosened the rope round her neck. And when the poor woman was lying on the ground—then we saw the most dreadful sight of all. He ripped out the golden pins with which her clothes were fastened, raised them high above his head, and speared the pupils of his eyes. "You will not see," he said, "the horrors I have suffered and done. Be dark forever now—eyes that saw those you should never have seen, and failed to recognize those you longed to see." Murmuring words like these he raised his hands and struck his eyes again, and again. And each time the wounded eyes sent a stream of blood down his chin, no oozing flow but a dark shower of it, thick as a hailstorm.

These are the sorrows which have burst out and overwhelmed them both, man and wife alike. The wealth and happiness they once had was real while it lasted, but now—weeping, destruction, death, shame—name any shape of evil you will, they have them all.

CHORUS

And Oedipus—poor wretched Oedipus—has he now some rest from pain?

MESSENGER

He is shouting, "Open the doors, someone: show me to all the people of Thebes, my father's killer, my mother's"—I cannot repeat his unholy words. He speaks of banishing himself from Thebes, says he will not remain in his house under the curse which he himself pronounced. But he has no strength: he needs someone to guide his steps. The pain is more than he can bear.

But he will show you himself. The bolts of this door are opening. Now you will see a spectacle that even his enemies would pity.

94

[*Enter Oedipus from door, blind.*]

CHORUS

O suffering dreadful for mankind to see, most dreadful of all I ever saw. What madness came over you? What unearthly spirit, leaping farther than the mind can conceive, swooped down on your destiny? I pity you. I have many questions to ask you, much I wish to know; my eyes are drawn towards you—but I cannot bear to look. You fill me with horror.

OEDIPUS

Where am I going? Pity me! Where does my voice range to through the air? O spirit, what a leap you made!

CHORUS

To a point of dread, too far for men's ears and eyes.

OEDIPUS

Darkness, dark cloud all around me, enclosing me, unspeakable darkness, irresistible—you came to me on a wind that seemed favorable. Ah, I feel the stab of these sharp pains, and with it the memory of my sorrow.

CHORUS

In such torment it is no wonder that your pain and mourning should be double.

OEDIPUS

My friend! You are by my side still, you alone. You still stay by me, looking after the blind man. I know you are there. I am in the dark, but I can distinguish your voice clearly.

CHORUS

You have done a dreadful thing. How could you bring yourself to put out the light of your eyes? What superhuman power urged you on?

OEDIPUS

It was Apollo, friends, Apollo, who brought to fulfillment all my sufferings. But the hand that struck my eyes was mine and mine alone. What use had I for eyes? Nothing I could see would bring me joy.

CHORUS

It was just as you say.

OEDIPUS

What was there for me to look at, to speak to, to love? What joyful word can I expect to hear, my friends? Take me away, out of this country, quickly, take me away. I am lost, accursed, and hated by the gods beyond all other men.

CHORUS

I am moved to pity by your misfortunes and your understanding of them, too. I wish I had never known you!

OEDIPUS

A curse on the man who freed my feet from the cruel bonds on the mountain, who saved me and rescued me from death. He will get no thanks from me. I might have died then and there; but now I am a source of grief for myself and all who love me.

CHORUS

I wish it had turned out that way, too.

97

OEDIPUS

I would never have become my father's killer, never have been known to all men as my own mother's husband. Now I am godforsaken, the son of an accursed marriage, my own father's successor in the marriage bed. If there is any evil worse than the worst that a man can suffer—Oedipus has drawn it for his lot.

CHORUS

I cannot say you made the right decision. You would have been better dead than blind.

OEDIPUS

What I have done was the best thing to do. Don't read me any more lessons, don't give me any more advice. With what eyes could I have faced my father in the house of the dead, or my poor mother? I have done things to them both for which hanging is too small a punishment.

Do you think I longed to look at my children, born the way they were? No, not with these eyes of mine, never! Not this town either, its walls, its holy temples of the gods. From all of this I am cut off, I, the most nobly raised in Thebes, cut off by my own act. It was I who proclaimed that everyone should expel the impious man—the man the gods have now revealed as unholy—and the son of Laius. After I had exposed my own guilt—and what a guilt! —do you think I could have looked at my fellow citizens with steady eyes?

No, no! If there had been some way to block the source of hearing, I would not have held back: I would have isolated my wretched body completely, so as to see and hear nothing at all. If my mind could be put beyond reach of my miseries— that would be my pleasure.

O Cithaeron, why did you receive me? Why did you not take and kill me on the spot, so that I should never reveal my origin to mankind?

O Polybus, and Corinth, and the ancient house I thought was my father's—what a handsome heir you raised up in me, how rotten beneath the surface! For now I am exposed—evil and born in evil.

O three roads in the deep valley, you oak wood and you narrow pass where the three roads meet, you who soaked up my father's blood, spilled by my hand—do you remember me? Do you remember what I did there, and what I did when I came here?

O marriage, marriage! You gave me birth, and then bred up seed from the one you brought into the world. You made an incestuous breed of father, brother, son—bride, wife, mother—all the most shameful things known to man.

But I must not speak of things that should never have been done. Quickly, in God's name, hide me somewhere outside Thebes, kill me, throw me into the sea, where you will never see me again.

Come close to me. I am a man of sorrow, but take courage and touch me. Do not be afraid; do what I ask. The evil is mine; no one but me can bear its weight.

[*Enter Creon, from side, with attendants.*]

CHORUS LEADER

Here is Creon. He will listen to your request. Decision and action are up to him, now that he has taken your place as the sole ruler of Thebes.

OEDIPUS

What shall I say to him? What justification, what grounds for trust can I present? In everything I did to him before, I have been proved wrong.

CREON

I have not come to mock you, Oedipus, nor to reproach you for the wrong you did.

[*To attendants*] If you have no respect for the feelings of human beings, at least show reverence for the sunlight which nourishes all men. Do not leave him there in full view, an object of dread and horror which appalls the holy rain and the daylight. Get him into the palace as fast as you can.

[*The attendants move over to Oedipus, and stand by him until the end of the scene.*]

Only his family should see the family shame; this public spectacle is indecent.

OEDIPUS

In God's name—since you have exceeded my hopes and come in so generous a spirit to one so low—do something for me. I ask it in your interest, not mine.

CREON

What is it you are so anxious to have me do?

OEDIPUS

Banish me from this country as fast as you can

—to a place where no man can see me or speak to me.

CREON

You can be sure I would have done so already, but first I wanted to ask the god Apollo what should be done.

OEDIPUS

But his command was clear, every word of it; death for the unholy man, the father-killer.

CREON

That *is* what the oracle said. But all the same, in our situation, it is better to inquire what should be done.

OEDIPUS

Will you consult Apollo about anyone as miserable as I?

CREON

Yes, and this time, I take it, you will believe what the god says.

OEDIPUS

Yes. I command you—and beg you—the woman in the palace, see to her burial. She is your sister, you are the man to do this. As for me, do not condemn this city of my fathers to shelter me within its walls, but let me live on the mountain, on Cithaeron, forever linked with my name, the mountain which my mother and father while they still lived chose as my burial place. Let me die there where they tried to kill me.

And yet I know this—no disease or anything else will destroy me. Otherwise I would never have been saved from death in the first place. I was saved —for some strange and dreadful end.

Well, let my destiny go where it will. As for my children, do not concern yourself about the boys, Creon. They are men; and will always find a way to live, wherever they may be. But my two poor helpless girls, who were always at my table, who shared the same food I ate—take care of them for me.

What I wish for most is this. Let me touch them with these hands, as I weep for my sorrows. Please, my lord! Grant my prayer, generous man! If I could hold them I would think I had them with me, as I did when I could see.

[*Antigone and Ismene are led in from the door by a nurse.*]

What's that? I hear something. Oh, God. It is my daughters, weeping. Creon took pity on me, and sent them to me, my dearest ones, my children. Am I right?

CREON

Yes, you are. I did this for you knowing the joy you always took in them, the joy you feel now.

OEDIPUS

Bless you for it! May you be rewarded for sending them. May God watch over you better than He did over me.

Children, where are you? Come here, come to these hands of mine, your brother's hands, the hands that intervened to make your father's once bright eyes so dim. Blind and thoughtless, I became your father, and your mother was my mother, too. I weep for you—see you I cannot—when I think of your future, the bitter life you will lead, the way men will treat you. What gatherings will you go to, what festivals, without returning home in tears, instead of taking part in the ceremonies?

And when you come to the age of marriage, who will take the risk, my daughters, and shoulder the burden of reproach which will be directed at my children—and yours? No reproach is missing. Your father killed his father. He sowed the field from which he himself had sprung, and begot you, his children, at the source of his own being. These are the reproaches you will hear. And who will marry you? There is no one who will do so, children; your destiny is clear—to waste away unmarried, childless.

Creon, you are the only father they have now, for we who brought them into the world are both of us destroyed. Do not abandon them to wander husbandless in poverty: they are your own flesh and blood. Do not make them equal to me and my miserable state, but pity them. They are children, they have no protector but you. Promise me this, noble Creon, touch me with your hand to confirm your promise.

And you, children—if you were old enough to understand, I would have much advice to give you. But as it is, I will tell you what to pray for. Pray that you may find a place where you are allowed to live, and for a life happier than your father's.

CREON

You have wept long enough. Now go inside the house.

OEDIPUS

I must obey, though it gives me no pleasure.

CREON

Yes, everything is good in its proper place and time.

OEDIPUS

I will go in then, but on one condition.

CREON

Tell me what it is. I am listening.

OEDIPUS

You must send me into exile—away from Thebes.

CREON

What you ask for is a gift only Apollo can grant.

OEDIPUS

But I am hateful to the gods above all men.

CREON

In that case, they will grant your request at once.

OEDIPUS

You consent, then?

CREON

It is not my habit to say what I don't mean.

OEDIPUS

Then take me away from here at once.

CREON

Come then, but let go of the children.

OEDIPUS

No, don't take them away from me.

CREON

Don't try to be master in everything. What you once won and held did not stay with you all your life long.

[*The following speech, for reasons too technical to discuss here, is considered by many authorities to be an addition to the play made by a later producer. The translator shares this opinion, but the lines are printed here for those who wish to use them.*]

CHORUS

Citizens who dwell in Thebes, look at Oedipus here, who knew the answer to the famous riddle and was a power in the land. On his good fortune all the citizens gazed with envy. Into what a stormy sea of dreadful trouble he has come now. Therefore we must call no man happy while he waits to see his last day, not until he has passed the border of life and death without suffering pain.

Look for these popular titles from Washington Square Press at your bookseller now

Graham Greene

___ **THE END OF THE AFFAIR**

"One of the best, most true and moving novels of my time, in anybody's language"—William Faulkner.
44535-9/$2.95/240 pp.

___ **THE HONORARY CONSUL**

A compelling tale of political intrigue and heartfelt passion by "the finest living novelist, bar none, in our language"—Harper's.
47271-2/$3.95/320 pp.

___ **ORIENT EXPRESS**

A stunning novel of violence and psychological intrigue.
43514-0/$2.75/256 pp.

Joan Didion

___ **PLAY IT AS IT LAYS**

At the center of this powerful novel is Maria, a young actress caught off balance by Hollywood, her husband, her hopelessly retarded daughter—and most of all, herself.
49590-0/$3.95/266 pp.

___ **RUN RIVER**

An unforgettable novel from one of America's most elegant and brilliant writers.
44258-9/$2.95/256 pp.

 WSP

WASHINGTON SQUARE PRESS
Published by Pocket Books

POCKET BOOKS, Department WSP 3B
1230 Avenue of the Americas, New York, N.Y. 10020

Please send me the books I have checked above. I am enclosing $_____ (please add 75¢ to cover postage and handling for each order. N.Y.S. and N.Y.C. residents please add appropriate sales tax). Send check or money order—no cash or C.O.D.'s please. Allow up to six weeks for delivery. For purchases over $10.00, you may use VISA: card number, expiration date and customer signature must be included.

NAME _____

ADDRESS _____

CITY _____ STATE/ZIP _____

☐ **Check here to receive your free Pocket Books order form.**